# A Rebel for Her Time

## a novel by
## Marie Mossman

Cover image: Rebekah Wetmore

Editor: Andrew Wetmore

ISBN: 978-1-7772937-4-1
First edition October, 2020

397 Parker Mountain Road
Granville Ferry NS
B0S 1A0

moosehousepress.com
info@moosehousepress.com

We live and work in Mi'kma'ki, the ancestral and unceded territory of the Mi'kmaq People. This territory is covered by the "Treaties of Peace and Friendship" which Mi'kmaq and Wolastoqiyik (Maliseet) People first signed with the British Crown in 1725. The treaties did not deal with surrender of lands and resources but in fact recognized Mi'kmaq and Wolastoqiyik (Maliseet) title and established the rules for what was to be an ongoing relationship between nations. We are all Treaty people.

This is a work of fiction, set among very real places and very real events. The author has created the characters, conversations, interactions, and many of the events, and any resemblance of any character to any real person is coincidental.

The author is not a doctor, and does not recommend following any medical procedures described in this work. They are fictional accounts of what may have taken place during World War 1, over a hundred years ago. For medical advice, consult a qualified medical practitioner.

Dedicated

to

doctors, nurses, and other essential workers

# Contents

# 1: Getting grown

Yes, the Deacon threatened me, but why did I complicate my life with the war and Charlie?

Queen Victoria reigned as I entered the world on 1875 in the cosy space known as the borning room of my family's salt box house in the village of East Cove, Nova Scotia. Father farmed and fished for our food. Mother cared for my eight older siblings as well as me.

I helped my parents with chores as I grew able. I scrubbed, weeded the garden, turned the drying cod, picked wild strawberries, blueberries and cranberries as the seasons brought them along, and assisted in the making of preserves. No supermarkets in those days. I learned the home remedies popular at the time. Yes, I wore a salt herring poultice around my neck to cure a sore throat, and dosed with sulphur and molasses as a spring tonic. I was academically gifted but a wilful child, perhaps spoiled because my older brother had died in infancy.

A neighbour man who used to visit our home was was appointed Deacon in the church. All the adults referred to him as the Deacon.

When I was twelve years of age, he came to our back door one day. I was alone in the house and Mother was in the garden choosing the beans she wanted to pickle. I answered the door. "Hi Del, my but you're getting tall. I bet you could reach the top of the doorway."

"Don't think so, Mr. Deacon."

"Give it a try. Stretch up." He grabbed me around the waist. "Reach up."

"I want to go down!"

"Sure." He put me down. His eyes were glazed and he shook his head.

"Mother's in the garden if you want to see her." I struggled to stop my voice sounding shaky.

"Yes...yes." He turned and walked away, toward the garden.

Another time, I was putting bread and jars away in our tiny pantry, when he visited. Mother, in the adjoining kitchen, greeted him.

"I noticed your tomatoes. They look delicious and you have so many. We can't ever grow a decent crop of them."

"Deacon, I'll run out right now and pick a bundle for you to take home."

"Don't bother yourself."

The second she headed out the door, he strolled into the pantry. He stood close and put his hand on mine. I tried to pull it away, but he tightened his hold. I froze, hand limp, face as blank as I could make it. He was blocking the doorway to the kitchen. I took in shallow breaths.

"Del, I've been wanting to talk to you about reading to the junior Sunday school class." He dropped my hand and returned to the kitchen at the sound of Mother's footsteps. My body shuddered.

By the time I was fourteen years of age, the mirror affirmed I was comely in a plain sort of way, with a peaches and cream complexion. My long hair shone golden specks only the day it was washed. I reached my full height of five feet three inches and had a slim build with fine bones. I compared myself unfavourably to my cousin, Charlene, with her dark good looks, always dressed in the latest fashion. She was my best human friend and only confidant in our village, now that my older cousin, Katherine, had moved to Boston.

Mother had promised me a new summer dress from the catalogue and when I tried it on, it had all the puffiness in the sleeves I'd been dreaming of. "I'll show my dress to Blackie," I told Mother as I passed her in the kitchen. She forbade me, so I stamped my foot and ran out the door.

Blackie was my best friend, my horse. Ah, the blue sky and fresh air in Nova Scotia on such a day. The scent of the sea outdoors, and then, in the barn, the smell of clean straw and fresh manure. I twirled and danced around, and hugged Blackie. "Like my dress, Blackie?" I made eyes at him and produced a pout.

I was about to move a shovelful of muck when the Deacon came in. He was old, maybe forty years old. He wore his go-to-town jacket and trousers.

"Saw you come here, all dressed up, Del. You're getting grown." He walked toward me. His eyes squinted. His lips curved up a little.

"You need something, Deacon? Going to a meeting?"

"Yeah…later. I like to help a girl your age…learn." His voice trailed off and his right hand went down toward his crotch. He started to unbutton the fly of his trousers. I froze.

He pulled out his penis and rubbed it. Ugly. Sticking out.

"Have to go," I tried to get past him.

He caught me by my dress. "Our secret. To help you."

Blackie neighed.

"Please, Deacon."

I grabbed the mucking shovel. A downward thrust hit the top of his shiny shoe.

"You bitch!"

I ran out of the barn, toward the house, and through the kitchen. Mother was too busy scrubbing a pot to notice. I continued up the stairs to my room. I cried, as quietly as I could, and stayed there, alone until near suppertime. I dabbed my eyes with a damp cloth before going down to set the table.

Sunday, before church, she asked about the mend on my sleeve. "I tore it in the barn when I showed my dress to Blackie. Sorry, Mother. I shouldn't have worn it out there."

My eyes teared up and I couldn't look straight at her. There was no use telling about the Deacon in the barn. Nobody would believe anything wrong about him.

I wondered what story he made up when he asked his wife to clean muck from his good trousers? After the barn incident, his eyes squinted ever so subtly whenever I noticed him looking at me.

Once, he whispered, "Sometime," and winked.

I became nervous about being alone, but sometimes was careless. I'd forget about the Deacon and then, he'd appear when I was alone outdoors, try to corner me.

**Marie Mossman**

# 2: I resolved

I was sitting in the sun outdoors and dozed off one afternoon, August of the same year.

*It seemed as if Mother wanted to make blueberry grunt. "We need a few more quarts."*

*We hadn't made grunt yet that year and I loved it more than anyone. "I'll get some extra. There's lots in the field over the hill."*

*I grabbed a container, maybe a pail, and headed out back, along the path and through scrub spruce. I hummed to myself and sang like an angel. No one was around to hear my tuneless music. I listened to late summer crickets and the greedy seagulls that feasted on berries. I enjoyed the special scent of the barrens, a mixture of spruce, rhododendron and juniper. I picked a few huckleberries to vary the task, as I usually did. Mother wouldn't mind.*

*I turned to go back with my pail and caught sight of a man hiking apace down the path in my direction.*

*Not him!*

*I ducked behind some bushes and raced, zigzagging this way and that, adrenaline powered, toward home. I couldn't see, then could see, or hear the Deacon pushing through the scrub bushes as he tried to follow my route. I flew the last few yards.*

I took a cautious amount of grunt at dinner. The sauce didn't taste as sweet as usual.

My mind fought the image of the Deacon puffing through the bush in pursuit of me. I resolved again not to be caught alone. If only someone would believe me if I told on him. But he was the Deacon. He collected money for missionaries and the Poor House. Most men didn't want to take on such responsibilities.

"Why are you so quiet lately?" Father would ask, but I never could explain to him.

The clincher came in the fall. "It's time we bred our lead cow, or we'll be getting short of milk next winter. This time you can watch, Della. It'll do you good to know how it works," Father announced.

I'd always been told to stay away when the cow was bred, so was eager to see the action.

The next time the moon was in the right phase for breeding, Father put our favourite Guernsey in the near pasture. I liked to pat the soft hair on our cow's hide. She was docile, always easy to milk and a good mother to her calf.

An uncle brought his bull over. The beast had horns that could impale a schooner's side, let alone any mere human or farm animal. The bull wasn't after wounding the cow, though. I didn't have to search to see its prong of a penis stick out beneath its rump.

When the bull mounted our cow, I looked away.

I saw the Deacon's penis sticking out of his trousers. At least I had managed to bang the shovel down on his foot. I had focused on his foot. The rest was too ugly.

"Look, Del, that's what it's all about," Father said.

The full force of the Deacon's intention stole my breath, shuddered through my chest.

"It's not something to cry about, Del. It's how life is made."

I threw up.

*Wish I was grown up. I'd move away.*

# 3: Our school

I remember how proud Father was when he announced, "Del, one of the Trustees asked if you'd teach our school come fall, seeing as you're all done yourself. I told him you surely would, if the board asked you. There you are, now, all fixed up with a job, and you're only sixteen!"

I knew Father wouldn't stand for me to back out. He had spoken for me. I was trapped in East Cove.

I decided to keep my ears and eyes open and tell my friends I was interested in trying another school the next year. Surely something would come up.

A letter arrived from the East Cove Trustees within days.

> *We are pleased to offer you a position to teach grades one to eight at our new East Cove Common School for the year 1891-92 at a salary of $158.43. In addition, you are expected to instruct students who may wish to follow the three year High School curriculum, make the fire on cold mornings, maintain the school and its grounds in a clean, tidy condition, and provide other services as the Trustees consider appropriate.*
>
> *We are informed your examination marks are the highest in Nova Scotia this year; therefore, the Board, after much debate, has agreed to increase your salary to $160.00 for the year, on presentation of documentation to confirm this matter.*
>
> *Signed,*
> *President of the Board of Trustees for the East Cove Common School.*

I had a job with a salary! I'd be able to order from the catalogue without asking Mother! I wondered if I'd need to buy chalk.

"Teaching's not always easy," Mother cautioned.

"But, Mother, I love math, reading, writing and pretend-teaching with children. It's as easy as snapping beans."

I was proud of our school. In its one room, it had two-person bench seats, windows, a cast iron stove in the middle, and a real blackboard, not just a painted wall to write on. I imagined myself in front of the room, the benches full of smiling faces intent on hearing my instructions. The children would stand when I entered. We would recite the Lord's Prayer, and sing "God Save the Queen" and "The Maple Leaf Forever". I would be kindly, beloved by all my students.

"Could you possibly unscrew the desks from the floor so we can move them easily for different activities?" I asked the trustees.

"Are you sure you want them off?"

"Yes, it'll be much easier when we have concerts."

My mind went blank when leading the Lord's Prayer the first day of school. I followed the children's recitation.

A couple of children had no spellers. An older boy showed up without a slate. "Mother needs the money to buy food," he said.

One senior student, only one, came with a slate and all the textbooks for the year. I asked the children who had a slate or a text to share with the others, but it was difficult for more than one child to read a book at the same time. Those who couldn't see the print well invented distractions, such as pinching a seat mate, to amuse themselves. How was I to get through a year of their larks?

I had never paid much attention to pranks when I was a student, though I knew they were going on. It didn't make sense to me to antagonize the teacher, but young boys felt differently. Day two of my teaching career, slate pencils started rolling down the slanted desks and falling off.

A hand went up: "Miss, my pencil won't stay still." Giggles all around.

"There's a groove at the top of your desk. Keep your pencils there."

I tried not to give attention to their petty tricks. The tallest youth used his knees to swing his desk back and forth above the floor. Another fellow moved his desk just enough to lower the legs onto the toes of a younger boy. I wished I had left the desks fixed to the floor.

Rumours abounded about nastier pranks planned for Hallowe'en. I let the children know how lucky they were to have a school. I praised all the families that had contributed to the building. I pointed out the work done to add little touches—a book shelf here, a bit of white washing there, a homemade bucket from a dirt-poor family. The rumours continued, but the day after Hallowe'en, our building stood, as pristine as ever, a monument to the children's pride in their school. I thanked God the school hadn't been burnt down.

One chilly morning, smoke billowed out of the stove and filled the classroom. Had a bird made a nest in the stovepipe the night before?

I kept the children outside until the fire burned down and the room aired out. I noticed two boys looking pleased with themselves. These brothers were both taller than me. As we discovered no nest, I concluded someone had blocked the pipe to create excitement at school.

Word went home to the parents to question their children. The next day, the two lads, chastened, came to me. "Sorry, Miss, about the stove pipe."

They handed me a note from their father. "I've already used the strop at home."

I restrained my urge to smile, pointed to the piece of branch in the corner, and replied, "Don't let it happen again, boys." I felt grateful to the parents who had supported me, and thanked them at church on Sunday.

Fear of the Deacon lurked under my composed exterior. I would arrive at school shortly before the children, leave with the last students and prepare my lessons for the next day at home.

I was the only daughter still living at home, and had a paying job, so Mother and Father let me keep the girls' room for myself. How I enjoyed the privacy! I spent most of my free time there, in lesson preparation, studying, and thinking of ways to look for a new teaching post.

I made a list: tell Mother, our priest, my friends; keep my ears open; read the newspaper; talk to people at a dance.

I avoided going to the barn, on walks, or anywhere else alone.

"What's gotten into you?" Father would ask.

"I have a lot of preparation and marking every day." I thought too often of the Deacon's evil intentions.

# 4: Mum's the word

"Will you walk me to the dance at the Anglican Church Hall Saturday evening?" I asked Daniel, one of my older brothers.

"Del, when are you gonna to grow up? Don't be such a scaredy cat. What's to be afraid of, walking up the road in daylight?"

"Please. I'll probably have someone see me home." I knew that, after the dance, Dan would prefer to see his own girlfriend to her house.

We headed up the road in time to arrive at the hall by eight o'clock. "It sounds like Edward's fiddling," I said. "I'm glad he's playing this evening."

Inside the hall, I enjoyed watching our pianist's fingers flit along the keys. She was eighty-two years old. I wondered if I would be so lively at her age.

I noted the banjo player strumming his instrument, which hung from his shoulder by a leather strap. His fiddle waited on the chair beside him.

George joined in with his accordion. We were lucky our musicians played for only the love of playing. I wished for a crumb of their talent.

The new wood stove from the Lunenburg Foundry stood unlit, as it was a warm evening for late September. Already, a group of young and old were step-dancing on the bare wooden floor. It didn't take many to fill a room of thirty by forty feet. Body odour from farmer-fishermen, who didn't take a Saturday bath, mixed with lavender and rosewater worn by women. The combination was an olfactory effect unique to a seaside community.

"Della, you came. I'm so glad." I turned to see Charlene walking through the door. She wore a dress with a pleated bodice, sleeves puffed near the shoulder, but fitted on her forearm. My dress had the puffed sleeves but lacked the pleated bodice.

"I haven't seen pleating like that before. It's lovely on you."

Charlene's mother ran the post office and a grocery store out of their front room, and Charlene had helped there since she had finished school. The older woman exchanged a bit of local news with each customer, just like she traded eggs for butter. I imagined she possessed a power to divine newsworthy contents in sealed envelopes when they passed through her hands.

"How's work going in the store?"

"Good. It's work, though. When there are no customers, Mom has me scrubbing in the store or in the house. I don't mind 'cause I like things extra clean, too, but it wears one down."

"There's something I want to ask you, Char...."

"This will be 'The Melrose'. We can take one more couple," Edward announced.

"Will you be my partner for this one?" A deep voice interrupted Charlene and me. George took my hand.

"See you after," I told Charlene as George tugged me toward the group forming a square.

"Hurry," he said.

"I'm not sure of all the steps."

"Just follow along."

We slipped into the remaining spot. Edward drew his bow across the strings to play a couple bars, then other musicians joined in. I marvelled how they played without printed music. No one called the dance steps.

George and I warmed up by step-dancing on the spot. Older couples knew the dance by heart, so I followed their movements. George and I, with another couple, faced two other couples. We eight stepped to the centre and back to our starting positions; then, four other couples did the same movement, starting from the other sides of the square. We continued with variations of meeting and turning, changing partners, making an archway. Finally, I ended beside George in our original position. We never stood still because we step-danced on the spot while others changed position. I thought it beautiful, how it worked.

I returned to the side of the hall where Charlene was chatting with other young women."Did you hear? I know but... I read in the paper..." I listened to the gossip, though resisted believing the worst of it.

A regular dance attendant who had eighty years behind him came over with his inevitable invitation. I didn't want to hurt the old fellow's feelings, so accepted—and could hardly keep up to his quick stepping around the hall.

Afterwards I stopped by another small group of young women. "Those fellows have been outside several times," I commented.

"Yes. Each time they come in, they're more rowdy."

"They keep nudging each other, looking at Charlene, and snickering."

We tensed when we saw the younger lad swagger over to Charlene. "Wanna dance?"

She hesitated, then the older boy joined the conversation. Nudges progressed to not-so-gentle pushes. I relaxed when one of the adult men said. "You fellers settle your problem outside. Let the young lady be."

"Those two fellows always have niggled each other like a couple of brothers," I said to a friend.

"Don't tell anyone I said so, but from what I hear, they've the same father," she confided.

"Explains a lot. Excuse me, I should have a word with Charlene about something else."

Charlene greeted me with her dimpled smile. "What was on your mind before George dragged you off?"

"Let's go sit for a minute in the corner," I replied.

"So, what was it?"

"Char, you have people coming in to the shop every day, so you get the latest news. I only see the school kids and my family, and I often miss information that would interest me. If you learn of any teaching posts, will you let me know?"

"Of course. I probably would anyway."

"Mum's the word. I don't want to upset anyone. I'd like experience away from here. The older boys give me such a hard time, maybe 'cause I've known them since we were in first year Sunday School together. If it's just as bad elsewhere I'll know teaching's not for me. Promise not to tell anyone?"

"Best friends, remember?"

"Thanks, Char. I feel like crying." I wanted to tell her about the Deacon as well, but couldn't, not at the dance. It never seemed the right time. Why?

"I didn't see you dance with George yet," I said.

Another young man offered his hand to me, and behind him strolled George who invited Charlene to dance with him.

Later, Edward put down his fiddle and came over to me. "May I walk you home this evening? We can leave early. I know your father wants you back by ten."

Edward, much older than me, was a real gentleman. "I'd like that, Edward. I'll tell Dan not to look for me later."

The music stopped. We could hear rowdiness out back of the hall. I knew if it wasn't the fellows who had vied for Charlene's favours earlier, it would be another pair emboldened by rum courage to spar. I wondered why men needed to fight.

# 5: Come in

I accepted Father's offer to travel with him as far as Easton on our horse-drawn wagon. "It would be a waste to pay the stagecoach when your mother and I need supplies from the store," Father explained. He would yarn with the storekeeper.

I planned to find another ride the remaining distance to Forest Plain, where I would be teaching at the Common School. I felt confident and knew I could prepare lesson plans quicker, with a year's experience behind me. I would escape the Deacon, make my own decisions.

I enjoyed the first minutes in silence as we rode the coastal road, beside a high fall tide, between mixed forest, and past fields of mature cabbages that were grown for sauerkraut. Father cleared his throat. "Del, I s'pose Mother told you how to protect yourself?"

"She gets so embarrassed 'bout everything."

"If anybody bothers you out the road, let them know they'll have to answer to me and your brothers."

"Would you believe me, Father?"

"Of course. Remember, you won't be so safe out the road as you are down home, where we men protect all the women."

"Oh."

"If a man corners you, you raise your knee sharply and hit him as hard as you can between the legs. No man can stand the pain. And run like hell. I can't be plainer. Understand?"

"Yes, Father." I understood he cared about me, and it was the right decision to leave home.

He tied the wagon outside and went into the familiar store to visit a while. A wheel of aged cheddar, coloured orange, was displayed behind the paying counter. Father bought a few things. "I'll take a pound o' your rat cheese if you don't mind, and do you have any o' your own bacon?"

"Yessir. Came over from the smokehouse yesterday."

"Then I'll take a pound o' bacon, too. Cut it thick. And, yeah, my wife wants a length o' cotton to sew a new pudding bag. Give me good stuff that's going to last a while, won't you? And if that young fella who does odd jobs is around, I'd like him to take my daughter up to Forest Plain."

*I could ask him myself.*

A farm lad, Thomas, carried my trunk to his wagon. The two horses harnessed to it snorted and pawed their hooves as if to say, "About time. Let's get going."

Father patted my shoulder. "You'll do well, Del." He turned to leave, then added. "Write."

I couldn't believe it. His eyes were damp.

As Thomas and I wended our way up the hill, I admired the countryside. I could have walked the distance, if not for my trunk. On my left was Easton Hill, a drumlin like many in Nova Scotia. The hill was mostly covered with spruce trees, except at the top, where a stately wooden house stood flanked by mature maples. After Easton Hill, the dirt road curved to our right as we passed a large shingled shed beside a modest home.

"What would that building be?" I asked.

"That's the ice house, Miss. If you can see, further down on the same side is a lake. When it's well frozen, the family who lives beside the lake cuts blocks of ice and stores 'em in the shed to sell in summer."

"Surely it melts in the heat."

"He covers it with lots of sawdust from the mill down below. That keeps the ice real good until 'bout September. Local folks are happy to pay for ice for picnics, and the rich summer people buy blocks regularly."

"There's a mill in Easton?"

"Yes, Miss, a river comes outta this lake."

We continued up a rise at a leisurely pace, then came to a divide in the road. To my left was a house that boasted a front veranda. Autumn perennials bloomed in front of the veranda and on the side within my view. The house was recently painted, and the semi-circular driveway had tidy edges. A general store, in paint to match the house, stood a few yards away. I wondered whether all the homes in Forest Plain looked as prosperous as this one.

The road branched to the left immediately after this store, but we continued straight up the hill to Forest Plain proper, the community where I was to board. I'd have to move from house to house until I'd been boarded by each family that enrolled children in school.

"Who are you boarding with first?"

"Mrs. John Jung. I take it there's no Mister."

"No, Miss, he's dead several months now. The family's scrub poor, but you'll find Mrs. Jung a good housekeeper, and they manage to get enough to eat. Grow most everything themselves. They's hard working people."

We passed a modest one-and-a-half storey on the right, and then a tiny bungalow on the left. All the houses were wooden, with shingles. Next up the hill on the left, I saw an unpainted house surrounded with debris, but my driver made no comment about it.

Across the road was a tidy building. I noted its neatly lettered sign, 'Forest Plain School'.

"There's your school, Miss. It's one year old now. The last teacher didn't stay the whole year. Teachers are hard to find, so folks are excited you're coming."

Thomas pointed to the house uphill and next to the school. "That there, Miss, is my house. We's twelve kids. I'm the oldest. If you last, you'll be boarding with us later on."

"I look forward to it," I lied. His home, though much larger than the messy one across the street, didn't look any more cared for. Its barn leaned as though it had given up resisting the northeasters.

The lad pointed left and right as he identified two other houses onward up the hill, occupied by his uncle and an aunt, and their respective families. Finally, we reached the top of the rise. "We're here," he announced. "I'll carry your trunk in, Miss, and let Aunt Rachel know you're here."

"How much do I owe you?"

"I dunno. Whatever you think, Miss."

I took ten cents from my purse. "Is this okay?"

"Yes, Miss." His reply was firm, but I noted a flatness. He thought I should have paid more, even though he wouldn't have had anything else to do all afternoon.

We walked between two chestnut trees, then by flower gardens on either side of the front entrance. The flowers were protected by a low white picket fence.

I noticed my 'honoured guest' treatment. Friends and family never went to the front door. Asters and nasturtiums were still blooming, but most other flowers had already produced seeds. I guessed Mrs. Jung was letting the seeds dry before collecting them for over winter.

I followed my driver to the front door. He opened it, then knocked. "Aunt Rachel, I've got the new teacher, Miss Schwester," he hollered.

A short, skinny woman with a huge belly opened the door. "Come in, come in, Miss Schwester. Mrs. Jung turned her head to the lad. "Thank you for picking her up, Thomas. You may go home now." She didn't want him hanging around.

"I must needs take her trunk up."

"Junior can do that. Bye now." To me she said,"I'll take you to your room. You can bring your bag along."

She led me up bare wooden stairs and along a corridor to a tiny room in the northwest corner of the house.

"It'll be wonderful to have a room to myself for preparing lessons."

"Usually our oldest girl sleeps here, but she's away housekeeping up the road. Makes one less mouth to feed, if you know what I mean, and she might get a little money to help out here, at home."

"How old is she?"

"Thirteen. Now, I must go down and tend to the dyeing. I cut the good parts off an old coat and am dyeing them. There should be enough material to sew up a coat for Eva."

She walked off, led by her belly. Another child on the way.

I stood, alone, fascinated by the view. I saw a clear blue sky and a band of green spruce that stretched from the distant horizon, toward the house until it met a fenced pasture that wore its autumn mix of gold and green. Between the pasture, and toward the back of the house, lay a mown field scattered with haystacks. Closer to the house, vegetable gardens were laid out, and next to the house was a narrow picketed flower garden. It mirrored the one that I'd passed to enter by the front door. I decided the Jungs were not really poor-whites, but flowers were the only luxuries in evidence. I thought widow Jung demonstrated great strength to maintain a flower garden and a pack of kids.

My eyes turned to immediate surroundings. The walls and floors of bare wood looked freshly scrubbed, and the bedding, though obviously well worn, was also clean. I had a table with a shallow drawer to function as a wash stand and a desk. An upended crate was the closest thing to a bureau. My clothing would remain stored in my trunk. The room was smaller, but otherwise about as luxurious as mine back home.

*A good start. I don't expect all the places are as clean as this.*

By the scent, I could tell Mrs. Jung had baked bread earlier in the day. I could have enjoyed a slab of bread and butter, if she had offered it. Luckily, the scent of something boiling, that was more appetizing than wool coat, indicated an imminent dinner.

I put the washbasin on top of the crate, my books on the shelves, and laid my writing paper on the table/desk. This would be home for the next month.

A child's hand tapped on my door, followed by a waif's voice. "Mommy says supper. Come."

I followed the girl along the corridor and down the stairs. I wondered how often children tumbled down the steep stairs.

The girl bubbled, "We're having a special dinner."

"Why would that be?"

"'Cause you're here, Miss. We're having rabbit. My brothers trapped 'em last night. Mom said everyone can have a piece of meat!"

I counted eight besides myself around the kitchen table, not far from the wood stove where the stew and wool scraps had simmered all afternoon. Mrs Jung introduced me to her oldest son, John Junior, named after his father. "We call him Junior most the time. He's the breadwinner, since his father died late last winter."

Then she ordered the rest of the children to say their names: Vernon, Fred, Ben, Eva, and the twins, Joe and Olive. "We're missing the oldest girl, like I told you, and the youngest, Mae. She's not eating supper 'cause of her temper fit this afternoon."

She picked up her ladle. "Junior, pass your plate. Then, you, Miss."

She ladled a goodly helping onto Junior's plate, less onto mine, and then served the younger children apparently by age. The serving size reduced quickly and everyone in the family was on the thin side.

"You said we'd all have meat," Eva whined.

"Just look, and you'll find meat. Junior, you show her the meat on her plate."

Mrs. Jung served herself last. All waited for her to pick up her fork and for Junior to say grace before they started.

"He makes us work in the fields all the time," Eva whined again.

Mrs. Jung retorted. "That's not true. I don't want to hear any more complaints. How do you think we're going to eat this winter if we don't get the crops in? You younger ones have plenty of time to play."

As in my family's home, conversation while eating was not encouraged, but here talking was even more limited. I wondered if my presence affected the family's interaction. The children all ate with one arm around their plate, as though to protect the contents from a neighbouring fork.

When Junior finished his stew, he took a piece of bread and wiped his plate with it before eating the bread. The others did the same. There was plenty of bread, but no butter on the table, and no milk jug.

My own reserved nature prevented me from introducing relaxed talk, and I doubted whether such efforts would have been appreciated. Widow Jung maintained pursed lips, except when she was putting food in her mouth.

As there was no hope of a second helping of stew, I decided to retire. "Mrs. Jung, thank you for a good supper. Now I must go prepare for school."

"You're welcome," replied Mrs. Jung. "The older boys'll work on the farm tomorrow. The twins and Mae stay home."

My first day of school at Forest Plain, the School Board Chairman introduced me.

I thanked him, then said, "Good morning, children. You look bright today, worthy of this beautiful school your parents have provided. If you study, you'll learn a great deal between now and summertime."

*The same curriculum as East Cove but I've a stronger hand than last year.*

"I'll work hard to help you, and I promise to treat you fairly. Now, bow your head for the Lord's Prayer."

I had them stand to join me in "God Save the Queen", then told them to sit. I led all the children in a brief oral review of basic addition facts. I assigned the older children written addition tasks from the blackboard, then started grade one pupils printing their numbers. While I was occupied with them, the Chairman nodded goodbye and left us to our work. Before recess, I introduced new spelling words and instructed the pupils to copy and study them while I cycled through the grades correcting the earlier arithmetic problems.

Outside during recess the children chased each other in games of tag, or tossed a ball, or amused themselves with games like hopscotch. I managed a trip to the outhouse before ringing the bell for class to resume.

I decided not to hear the odd excessive scraping on a slate, and worked on giving the bigger boys important jobs and avoiding an idle minute for anyone.

After recess, grades seven and eight were assigned a composition with the beginning, 'A weird thing happened to my neighbour last summer....' "Practise good penmanship for your story, and remember 'weird' and 'neighbour' are on your spelling list."

Grades two to six were to write at least one sentence about what they did during vacation time. When finished, they were to read the first story in their reader. I helped the grade one pupils work on printing and reading their names. Before lunchtime, I invited everyone to stand and sing the ABCs to help grade one learn the alphabet.

After lunch, I assigned the lower grades additional numbers or arithmetic practice while I introduced algebra to grade eight. Grades one and two practised printing or writing while grades five to eight began history. Then I encouraged grades one to seven to add items from their imagination while they drew from a large illustration I took from a magazine. I introduced grade eight to their first short sentence in Latin.

We ended our day with volunteers from the lower grades displaying and explaining their pictures. I had a few songs up my sleeve in case of restlessness, but the children participated enthusiastically, so I kept the songs for another day.

When I could finally dismiss class, I permitted my mind to muse on a pair of doves who occupied a branch within view of my desk. They sat together, like a caring couple.

*Will I ever find a true love?*

# Marie Mossman

# 6: Slippery chin

I abandoned the image of those peaceful doves to memory as soon as I arrived back at the Jung home. The children were running around like chickens surprised by a fox. "Mama peed all over the floor 'cause the baby's coming. You have to help."

"She doesn't want Thomas's mother 'cause they squabble."

"It's too late to get the doctor."

Mrs. Jung sat in her rocking chair. Tears leaked from her eyes. "It's early. Shouldn't be coming yet. Help me." This was not the woman of last evening.

"Mrs. Jung, I don't know how to deliver babies."

"I'll tell you what to do."

"I'll try."

"Junior, help me get your mother to the borning room." We tucked Mrs. Jung into bed.

"We'll need boiling water and the sharp kitchen knife," she said.

I delegated tasks the children could do. "Fred, take some bread for Joe, and the two youngest girls, and play with them outside. Keep them there. Vernon, you put the kettle and pots of water on to heat. And bring a clean sharp knife. Ben, keep the wood box full. Eva, go find some clean sheets, your mama's older ones, and some baby blankets. Junior, check Fred and the little ones are okay outside."

Eva arrived with a scattering of linen.

*Please, God, what am I supposed to do?*

I took Mrs. Jung's hand. "Junior's checking on Fred and the youngest children, and the older children are helping me. Tell me what we need next."

*How will I get lessons prepared for tomorrow? Will they blame me if something goes wrong? Keep calm. Should I have gotten Thomas's mother instead of agreeing? Calm.*

Mrs. Jung screamed. Then louder, and again. "Help! Up! Need t' push!"

Eva and I bolstered Mrs. Jung with pillows and struggled her upper body to a semi-upright position. She grunted animal-like sounds as she strained to push the baby out. I'd seen cats born, and a calf in the barn. Animals made less fuss than Mrs. Jung.

*Is birth always so hard for women?*

She was at it for at least an hour before she said, "It's coming out next push. Put the knife in the boiling water and don't touch nothing with it 'til I tell you."

The top of the head appeared, with dark hair. Mrs. Jung made an Amazon push. The whole head came out but the body was stuck.

I remembered what Father had said when he helped a cow deliver her calf. "It's important to get it out quickly."

I wiggled two fingers under the slippery chin, then pulled as Mrs. Jung pushed. The baby budged.

*Thank God.*

Two more pushes from her and I had a wrinkly, skinny, perfectly-formed infant in my hands.

"Make it cry. That'll clear its lungs," Mrs. Jung directed.

The wee thing didn't need encouragement. It cried on its own.

"Miss, cut off the cord. Make sure it's long enough to tie up real tight."

The cord was more slippery than a cooked noodle in water, but I managed.

"Make your mother comfortable with the pillows while I tend the baby," I told Eva.

I washed my hands of blood, cleaned and tidied the newborn.

*You really do need lots of water when a baby is born. Wish I could air the room. No window.*

I wrapped the child tightly like I'd seen mothers do.

"Mrs. Jung, another beautiful girl."

"I'll hold her a minute, then you put her on my stomach. That'll help the afterbirth come out."

"I couldn't have done it without your help, dear," I praised Eva. "You go tell the others they have a new sister. Joe and the girls can come in the house now, but not in here."

I looked in on Mrs. Jung. "Would you like some tea and bread?"

"Yes, Miss, thank you, and tell Eva to put out a cold supper for the children. I'll be up in the morning." She made a wan smile. "This was the easiest of all them."

I called out for Vernon to make a tray for his mother.

Once the borning room was tidied, I told Mrs. Jung. "I must stay up late to prepare lessons for tomorrow. May I use the oil lamp to work tonight?"

"Yes, Miss, but don't keep it on any longer than you have to. The oil costs."

My body sagged. I pulled myself to my full height and forced a smile. "Thank you."

In my dreams during the night, two doves flew toward a distant cloud of smoke.

**Marie Mossman**

# 7: First challenge

Mrs. Jung was in her rocking chair nursing the baby when I went down to the kitchen in the morning.

"I've named her Jean, a girl's form of John. That way, her father'll always be with her. And her middle name is Della. She'll know you're the kind lady who delivered her."

"I'm honoured." And I was.

I helped myself to yesterday's bread from the table. With a nod in the direction of the wood stove, Mrs. Jung said, "Tea's ready. Junior put it on earlier."

"Can you manage today, Mrs. Jung?"

"Eva knows how to start the bread. Vernon can come in later from the field to help her with kneading and the stove part. We bake bread every day here. I'm worried whether I can keep on top of the twins, though."

"Would it help if I took them to school, just for today? If the inspector comes by, I'm sure he'll understand, under the circumstances."

Off I went down the dirt road for my second day of school, weary, a vague plan in my head, and an urchin on either hand.

*Keep them too busy for mischief.*

By the time I rang the bell for the children to come into school, they knew why the twins were there. I had the pupils sit, then explained, "You were such sensible children yesterday, I'm sure you'll help me with Joe and Olive today. Each grade'll have a turn to do exercises with them as the day goes on. It's the first graders' turn now. Squeeze together to make room for Joe on one side of your bench, and Olive on the other. Good."

"Now, everyone stand and we'll show them how well we sing 'God Save the Queen.'"

I hummed the first note, and the children joined. Next, we recited the "Our Father". I heard my voice, strong and steady.

"Grade four, raise your hands. Joe and Olive, move up to grade four. Each of you in grade four read yesterday's story to one of the twins. If you finish that, try the next story. I'll be working with grade two on arithmetic. The rest of you, do problems from the blackboard. You may quietly help the person next to you, but you must stay in your seat."

I had everyone stand and recite the times tables, and then let all the children out for recess.

The youths played catch behind the schoolhouse where there was a clearing. It served as a playground for the children, and there were no windows to break on that side. Spruce trees on three sides created a natural boundary. The ball, and cleared area, comprised the total exercise equipment supplied by the trustees for our physical fitness program.

So far the older boys were model students. Would it last?

The younger children entertained themselves by playing Red Robin and Leap Frog, or by exploring scrub bushes, flowers, or insects on the playground. I surprised myself by smiling.

After recess a voice piped up, "Miss, you're supposed to be the teacher. I shouldn't have to show Olive how to print her name. I'm going to tell my uncle. He's the inspector."

*Not where I expected my first challenge.*

My jaw tightened. My stomach contracted. I smiled. I replied sweetly, "I'm glad you know the inspector, Priscilla. I look forward to his visit and his suggestions for improvements. When you show Olive how to print her letters, the practice will be good for your own printing. Do raise your hand if you need help." My voice firmed. "Now get started."

"Yes, Miss."

I asked children in the higher grades to write at least one correct sentence, and the pupils in the lower grades to copy a sentence from the day's reading. The children took turns reading their sentences aloud.

One lad caused great merriment with "Our dog rolled in the shit under the outhouse. He stinks."

Joe and Olive each named a favourite animal and told why they liked it. We all applauded their contribution.

I kept the twins separated and moved them frequently. "Would you like to take Joe out and play toss the ball with him for five minutes? You throw beautifully, and he could learn from you," I suggested to one of the teenage boys who was getting fidgety in the afternoon.

"Yes, Miss." He was out the door with Joe in a flash.

I introduced Canadian geography. "Who can tell me the western boundary of Canada?" A hand shot up. "Good," I said. "Grade eleven remembers from last year."

We continued with talk about who lives in Canada. I guided them to decide most of the people in Canada were of British or French background, and that our county included many people of German origin.

One child added. "The Mi'qmaq are here, too. Ma's afraid to hang wash on the clothesline in the night 'cause a Mi'qmaw might be out there."

I agreed we share our land with native people. *I don't think of that often enough.*

The school day was getting on, so I asked the children to copy their spelling words onto their slates to study for homework. Then I chose a few well-known songs from the *Bouquet of Kindergarten and Primary Songs*. The younger children went home cheerfully singing "Three Blind Mice".

I reviewed the day in my mind, how the older youths were co-operative so far, but Priscilla was a girl to keep under my thumb.

I wrote sums on the board for the next day, picked up my planning book, and expelled a weary sigh. "Come, Joe and Olive. Let's scurry home and see how Mother and Jean are getting on."

Marie Mossman

# 8: Letters

Over several years, my love of learning caught on with one or two star students. Junior Jung sought extra help, but providing for his younger siblings frequently kept him from class. His self-motivation led him to a construction business, not academics.

Lorne stood out among all my students. After grade school, he worked as a labourer, studied late by lamplight, and gained entry to Dalhousie University. He slept in a cheap rooming house and skimped on meals so he could buy books. I read in the newspaper that he became a lawyer.

I did cherish the one or two serious students like Junior, but the majority of boys and girls attended school because they had to. Most girls preferred the ready rewards of bread baking or preserving fruit, and I'd learned to brace myself to lose them once they were teenagers. They'd be sent to housekeeping jobs, or hastily married. Those who stayed in school spent more time flirting than concentrating on math or literature.

Boys wanted to test their strength and skills in the woods or barn. I continued to tear my hair out taming youths who merely amused themselves in school between absences. My personal "Look on the bright side" self-talk failed me more frequently as the years passed.

I ventured brief visits to East Cove for important holidays with my family. The blueberry nightmare usually recurred before a visit, and I came to dread it as I steeled myself to cope if I encountered the Deacon. How I wished to denounce the man, but I knew I would pay more than he if I spoke against him.

Charlene, who married George, had quickly become a devoted mother. Our friendship continued, though our interests diverged.

Each visit, Blackie would stretch his neck toward me in recognition. I'd brush him and give him treats. There would be a bit more grey hair on Mother's head, and Father would search for common words.

"Dan's taking over the farm," he told me as I left one time. We'll all live here and he'll take care of us. Don't you worry about Mother and me."

I wept during my return to Forest Plain. Why? I felt sad to see my parents failing, guilty for leaving them, grateful to Daniel.

*Be honest, Della, you also felt light, free.*

I opened *The Canadian Magazine* to relax at my desk after the children of Forest Plain were dismissed to a fresh spring day. I read, mused, longed for travel, or at least a different challenge, after ten years of teaching there, but I counted my blessings every morning. My independent profession with its salary was always included on the list.

Most women had less opportunity than I, but a subscription to *The Canadian Magazine* had broadened my interests and ambitions. The magazine covered politics, science, art and literature. I was excited by its pictures and descriptions of famous people and places. A recent article in its 'Woman's Sphere' had argued that our country would benefit if more women were educated to practise trades and professions. Social restrictions restrained a woman's potential. How could I break through to a better life?

My daydream was interrupted by Thomas, no longer the lanky youth who transported me up the hill from Easton on my arrival to Forest Plain. He delivered a letter from Mother.

I put it in my satchel to enjoy in the evening. I'd write my duty letter first.

> *March 22, 1901*
> *Dear Chairman, and all members of the Forest Plain School Board,*
> *Assisted by your unwavering support, I have enjoyed the privilege of teaching your children these past several years. They are an exceptional group of young people and I hope they have learned as much from me as I have from them. If you wish that I continue in this post for another school year, it is also my wish. I look forward to your reply at your earliest convenience.*
> *Yours respectfully,*
> *Miss Della Schwester*

I put this letter with Mother's in my satchel, tidied myself, and joined a group headed to town for Easton's Spring Fling.

The scent of frying sausages and the murmur of a crowd met me as I approached the flat piece of land reserved for community gatherings. After the youth band played "God Save the Queen," Easton's portly mayor orated on the importance of good citizenship, then declared the Fling open.

I was puzzled when Priscilla pushed her new baby and carriage toward me.

"Miss Schwester, I was hoping my wee one would benefit from your teaching like I did. It seems not."

I managed only a stunned, "Oh," before she turned and headed for the bake sale table.

Lorne's aging parents approached me for the first time ever. His father said. "We're sorry you're leaving. You were Lorne's best teacher."

I smiled. "Thank you for the kind words. You folks seem to know something I don't."

The local doctor cornered me and wanted to know my plans. "I've been worried you'd put me out of business with your delivering babies and patching up your youthful charges."

"Nothing to worry about, Dr. Smith. I just take care of my pupils' little accidents."

"Seriously, though, you should train for nursing. There aren't many medical schools that'll accept women who want to be doctors. I wouldn't recommend it to you anyway. It's a rough road."

"Lots of women work on farms. I think they're tough enough for doctoring. And when they get the chance to study, many prove as booksmart as men."

He had not listened. "You'd make a wonderful wife for some doctor, though." He paused. "Try nursing. I hear they have a school in Boston," wink, wink, "then come back and marry me."

"Thank you for the compliment, Doctor. You're right about the need for women to train for paying jobs. Most women aren't paid for their work."

"I quite agree, my dear. I feel sorry for a woman's lot in life."

"You agree they should be paid for their work, and have equal access to education?"

"Well, they're the weaker sex, and so need men to do the real jobs. Women are made differently, made to care."

"I don't want to argue with you at the Fling. Maybe I'll drop off my copy of *The Canadian Magazine*. You'd find interesting new thinking on economics and politics, if you took a look at the latest 'Women's Sphere' section."

"Yes, well, I don't have much time for reading a woman's magazine, you'll understand."

"It's been pleasant chatting, Doctor. If you'll excuse me, I must provide information to parents over there."

I walked over to a family that I knew and chatted briefly. Then, I bought sweets from the Anglican church fundraiser and enjoyed watching the older boys test their skills at ring toss or swing the hammer, ring the bell. They competed to win a plush toy or box of chocolates which the winner promptly gave to a girlfriend. Serious mothers, who would never consider themselves gamblers, gleefully played games of chance run by the men's lodge.

I employed my standard excuse of having work to do as I to slipped away early from the Fling. Once I was home, I settled down to read my mother's letter.

*March 21, 1901*
*My Dear Della,*

*I pray this letter reaches you in time and in good health. Has it been as cold in Forest Plain as here by the water, in East Cove?*

*Your cousin, Katherine, who lives near Boston, and who has longed for a baby, is once again expecting. If God wills, the infant will arrive in about six months. We are all so happy, yet anxious, for her and Frank. Because of her history, her doctor has ordered Katherine to bed, and to hire a practical nurse, which is beyond their means. They have asked if anyone in our family could help them, and I immediately thought of you. She may have hesitated to contact you directly because she thinks of you as a career woman, and she may not want to impede your success.*

*If you have not already signed your contract for another year, I beg of you to open your heart to Katherine. You were always good friends when she lived here. I think your successful experiences (delivering a baby, dressing wounds, pitching in with cooking and clean-up when needed) in the various families where you have boarded have given you the skills to run Katherine's home and to nurse her during her pregnancy. We've always believed family comes first.*

*Your father and I are keeping as well as expected. There's a new calf and the hens are broody. Dan and your other brothers help out here at home, so you needn't worry about going far away for a spell.*

*People around are proud of your accomplishments, and the Deacon, especially, takes an interest in how you are doing. The limp he developed when you still lived at home is more pronounced, but he is such a humble man, he never mentions it.*

*Be assured we care well for Blackie, your old pet.*

*Let me know what you think about helping Katherine while she is with child. I'm sure she will look for an early response.*
*Sincerely,*
*Mother and Father*

I wrote two letters that evening, and destroyed the one that I'd written to the board earlier in the day.

Fortunately, I managed a ride to town on Monday, the next day the post office was open. I wasn't bothered by our washboardy road, my spirits were so high, and my mind was occupied, envisaging my voyage to Boston.

My recurring nightmare, the one of racing for home from blueberry picking ahead of the Deacon, disturbed my sleep the night before I visited my parents.

The couple of days in East Cove with Mother and Father reassured me of their situation. Dan managed the heavier farm work, and my other brothers pitched in, under his leadership. Bertha, Dan's wife, cooked most of the meals, loaves and preserves.

I asked Mother about her habit of afternoon rest.

"Bertha tells me it's the latest innovation to assure a long life. She threatens to cut off her fresh bread if I don't lie down for a while. She's such a dear, I can't take a threat from her seriously, and I do feel perky after a rest."

I should have asked Bertha about the matter, but already my mind was set for adventure, a new direction.

**Marie Mossman**

# 9: Boston and Malden

On Tuesday, I boarded the stagecoach in East Cove, direction Halifax City, about forty miles away.

"Sit in the back, Miss. You're less likely to get motion sickness," the driver advised.

He stopped at Noble's Wharf in the city, and I walked the gangplank onto the new steamship *Halifax.* I had bought my ticket in advance as Katherine and Frank had sent me the $8.20 needed for the ship's fare.

"Welcome aboard, Miss," said the captain.

"Thank you, sir." I smiled. "You've arranged a smooth crossing, have you?"

"Agents are telling people so, but my barometer's falling. Can't promise anything, m'self."

"We'll keep our fingers crossed. You've a good reputation. If you'll excuse me, I should go below and settle in."

He doffed his cap to me, and I headed to my stateroom.

Later, I enjoyed dinner in the formal dining room. The head waiter asked. "Miss, would you prefer to dine by yourself, or with a group?"

I opted to dine with others. He led me to a table with a young married couple, two men in suits, and a tidily dressed woman.

The gentlemen stood until I was seated, then one of the single men said. "State where you come from and your reason for travel. It's the rule here."

His friendly, approving manner put me and everyone else at ease to share our information, though the husband of the couple spoke for himself and his wife. The other woman, I learned, was an Acadian from Grand Desert who was travelling to employment as a housekeeper. She contributed little conversation as her English was limited, but her smile added to the pleasant mood around the table.

Over our British-style dinner of roast beef and vegetables, our informal host had us vote on the likelihood of a storm. Result—four, no storm; two expected a storm.

Then he asked us, "Which is better, apple or cranberry pie? And why?"

With such light conversation, we became friends and only parted when no pie remained on our dessert plates. I envied his conversational skills.

The ship departed Wednesday morning, travelling via Yarmouth. Early Thursday morning, we ran into a fierce storm off the Maine coast.

I braved the rocking corridors to return to the dining room for a civilized breakfast, took one look at my plate of bacon and sunny-side- up eggs, and felt my stomach retch.

"Madame, we recommend a dry bun and black tea," the waiter said. "Be careful when you return to your stateroom. A man broke his arm in the corridor when the ship lurched."

I felt sorry for the man; however, the news lessened my embarrassment about seasickness. It wasn't as if I took pleasure in a stranger's bad luck, but my mood definitely benefited from his misfortune. I pondered whether Father would have called it *Schadenfreude*.

A ship's officer entered the dining room while I nibbled my bun and sipped my tea. "Ladies and gentlemen, the captain has asked me to assure you the storm will abate soon. It's heading for the Bay of Fundy. They usually do."

The *Halifax* arrived in Boston after approximately twenty-four hours of sailing. I disembarked wearing a red scarf, as I'd promised in a letter sent ahead.

"You're Miss Schwester? I'm Katherine's husband, Frank." He was about five feet, ten inches tall, and small boned for a man, less imposing than I had expected. He wore his dark hair cut short, with a part on the right side, and his well-groomed moustache reminded me of a miniature English toy spaniel.

"How kind of you to meet me right at the pier."

"Welcome to Boston! Did you have a pleasant crossing? Not seasick?"

"Yes, quite pleasant. I'm used to the sea."

"We're grateful you've come to help Katherine. Let me deal with your luggage, then I'll whisk you away 'cause Katherine's anxious to see you."

"I must thank you again for sending the ship's fare to me."

"Least we could do when you're leaving your teaching position to help us."

Frank's speech had a touch of French accent, and I'd been told his family immigrated to Chicago from Quebec. Frank had moved to Boston about the same time as Katherine. Adjusting to city life in Boston was their first common link. What he lacked in size, he made up for in his polite manner. Probably, it was his genuine politeness that had landed him his steady job as an elevator operator.

Frank had borrowed a wagon for our trip. He helped me with my bags, paid a porter to load my trunk, assisted me to my seat, and hopped up beside me.

"There's lots to see around Boston, but tonight we'll go straight home to Malden. Katherine's been looking forward to your arrival this evening. Tomorrow afternoon, you'll see more of Malden. Katherine has a few errands for you. That reminds me, while we're here at the dock, I'm s'posed to buy a jug of molasses. It's a good price, off a boat straight from Jamaica."

I felt a twinge of homesickness while Frank made his purchase of molasses. It had been a favourite treat of mine growing up.

"Boston looks busier than Halifax. What's the population?"

"About 550,000."

"That's three times as many!"

"Yes, growing every day. Malden is as modern as Boston. People are getting telephones! In my store you'll see the things people are buying. Katherine and I like the latest inventions, but we try not to spend too much. Wise to put something away with the baby coming, don't you think?"

"Of course. Tell me about your home."

"We've two rooms on the second floor of a boarding house. One room's for Katherine and me, and the other's furnished for you. They're nice. Each has a window. You'll see. Look off to the right, Della. See that large brick and stone building?"

"What is it?"

"It's called Faneuil Hall, after the man who gave money for the original building. Some controversial speeches have been made there."

"How so, controversial?"

"One man claimed blacks should be given the vote. Imagine!"

"Surely some of them could make a sensible choice. I can't vote in Canada, 'cause I'm a woman. That doesn't seem fair to me."

"But, Della, women are cared for by the men in their lives. If a girl isn't married, her father can vote, and a married woman has a husband who can vote."

I decided not to argue with Frank on my first day. "I'd like to visit Faneuil Hall sometime."

We continued northward for about fifteen miles until we entered Malden. Shortly afterwards, he pointed out a cemetery. "A couple dozen soldiers from the Revolution are buried there. More than a hundred years ago."

He turned onto Fraternal Avenue. "That two-storied wooden house, number 330, is home. I'll introduce you to our landlady, Mrs. Parnell. We call her Mrs. P. I'll take your luggage up, and then return the wagon to my friend."

Mrs. P. welcomed me effusively, but didn't stop there. "Next week's my turn to 'ost our 'ospital aide group. We supply the 'ospital with quality linens. Everyone'll be deliiiiiiighted to 'ave you join us. On Tuesday, we'll cut and baste sheetin' for pillow cases. Do come meet the ladies, whot's all quality people. Now run along upstairs, 'fore Katherine abandons 'er bed 'cause I've captured you."

Frank, who had returned by now, guided me up dark, balustraded stairs to Katherine. She lay in bed, a few unopened novels strewn at her side. I noted her thin face and pasty skin.

"Katherine!"

"Della, you're here!"

"Of course, dear. It's a grand adventure visiting you and Frank in Boston. I intend to fatten you up so you produce a plump baby come Christmas. How's that for a goal?"

"If you only can, Del."

"Let's start with a little something from home. Mother sent cocoa and a tin of her ginger cookies, so if Frank charms hot milk and sugar from Mrs. P., we can enjoy a mug-up while we chat. You have pleasant accommodations."

"I'll run down for the milk," Frank said.

"I mustn't go downstairs, doctor's orders," Katherine said. "So we're lucky the toilet is on the upper floor. In winter, we're allowed a hot bath once a week. There's no heating water on the stove like at home. It's all modern, more convenient."

When Frank returned with three steaming cups of milk on a tray, I quickly mixed up cocoa.

"These biscuits, Del, take me right back to East Cove. So friendly."

Frank offered to show me my room. It was eight by ten feet. The window looked out to the back yard and a mature elm. I had a slim bed, desk, small bureau and a hard chair at the desk, fitted with a cushion. My trunk fit under the bed, and hooks were installed where I could hang my dress and coat. The nine-patch quilt on the bed was from Katherine's childhood home, and I noticed the rug beside the bed as one hooked by her grandmother. Frank and Katherine had gone to trouble to furnish the room to an easterner's taste.

I returned to Katherine. "The room's perfect, so homey."

"Frank's the one who arranged it. I mostly supervised. Glad you like it."

"I visited your parents before leaving. Your mother keeps on pickling and baking, almost like when you all lived in the house at East Cove. She gives away the extras for church sales. I think she and Mother get together often for tea."

"And Daddy? How's he, really?"

"Doing well. Complains a bit about his right knee aching, but manages just as before. Your brothers help him with the heavier jobs. Your mother and father read and reread every letter from you, until the next one arrives."

"I can see it. I keep theirs."

"Kathy, are there other roomers here?"

"Yes, on our floor there are three other rooms. One's rented to a seamstress who works long hours at a shop. I think she's a relative of our landlady. Mrs. P.'s family uses the other two rooms. We're welcome to sit in the parlour downstairs. 'Course, now I'm in bed, Frank stays up here when he's home."

"How do you get meals?"

"Mrs. P. cooks. Frank brings a tray up to me, and he takes a packed lunch to work. It used to be friendly to eat with the family, but now I find the days long. It's going to be so much better with you here. I hope you like it, Della."

"You should rest now, Kathy. We'll chat again later."

"All right. Frank must go to work for the afternoon. He'll ask Mrs. P to put lunch for us on a tray for you to bring up, if you don't mind."

I smoothed Katherine's bedding, and left her to rest. It took little time to arrange my clothing and books.

I wasn't tired, so I wrote a note to Mother and Father. They'd expect one.

*Malden, Mass.*

*Dear Mother and Father,*

*I hope this short letter finds you as well as you were a couple of days ago. It's a comfort to know how helpful Dan and the others are around the farm. Is the new calf thriving as expected?*

*The Halifax is as sturdy and up to date as the newspaper reports. I'd never before been in a dining room as elegant as the one on the ship. Such luxurious draperies, with gold cords and tassels! And the cutlery—special items for fish, and soup, and dessert. I ordered a proper English roast beef dinner with Yorkshire pudding. It wasn't like dinner at home in the family, not as good as your roasts and pies.*

*The trip went well. There was a little bit of a blow off the coast of Maine, but the ship stood up to it. I think the Captain was well experienced and competent. Frank met me at the pier in Boston this morning and chatted in a friendly manner on the ride to Malden.*

*Katherine is resting at this moment. She is pale and mostly confined to bed, as a precaution. I think she is lonely, but her spirits should lift with company. As meals are prepared by the landlady, I'll take on other duties. Katherine and Frank appear to understand the importance of respect for her delicate condition. We'll do what we can to produce a healthy grandchild for her parents, and to improve Katherine's strength.*

*I'll end this letter by sending love to you.*

I heard a bed springs squeak in the other room so peeked in. Katherine beckoned me. I was happy to see her more animated.

"Shall I bring up our tray?"

She nodded, so I ran down and carried it to her room. I propped Katherine to a sitting position.

"While we eat, tell me more about your landlady."

"Mrs. Parnell's husband's a sea captain and often away. She's from England herself. Mrs. P. helps us as much as she can, but with two children to care for, her own housekeeping, and all her good works, she's little time to talk with me. Besides, she has a tendency to go on about how things are done more properly in England. It gets tiresome."

"What sort of good works does she engage in?"

"Her biggest project is collecting linens for the new hospital that'll be opening. She also has work parties at the house where ladies knit or sew clothing for new babies, or put together baby kits for poor mothers. The whole Boston area's flooded with immigrant families from Europe, and American farms, and needy single men and women. Mrs. P.'ll probably rope you into helping her with her work parties."

"Might be a way for me to meet some people. I see you have a Singer in the nook by the corner window. Do you sew so much you need a machine at home?"

"I was earning a tidy penny sewing lingerie. There are women who pay well for pretty underthings. I sew the seams with the machine, and add lace by hand."

"Don't you feel isolated, working alone at home?"

"No, but Frank doesn't like me talking about my work."

"Why not?"

"My clients are low class women. Anyone can tell by their talk. What I like is I can go to meetings and shop when I please and don't have to put up with a nasty boss or crude workmates. I don't like being confined to bed like this, but working here for myself is completely different. Frank lets me do what I want with the money I earn. Most men don't."

"I understand."

I wondered if I was up to guiding her when her time came. Katherine was no Mrs. Jung.

Frank arrived home for suppertime. We dined like a little family. He ate off a tray on one side of the double bed, and I on the other, with Katherine sitting up in the middle, bolstered by pillows.

"I hope, Della, you'll have time to visit the department store where I work."

"Maybe I could, on a day when Katherine feels better."

"I'll take you up in my elevator. Have you ever been on one?"

"Never. How does it work?"

"Cables pull the car up and let it down. Ours was built by the Otis Elevator Company and has their safety device. I've perfect confidence in it."

"It's wonderful, isn't it, all the inventions these days?" I said.

Our talk turned to my duties, and we agreed I'd help out as needed, with a major part of the help being companionship for Katherine.

# 10: Best options

I participated in one of Mrs. P.'s work parties the next week and could not have anticipated the tone of the conversation.

Fanny, a widow in her late seventies, was first to introduce her liberated opinions. "If we had the vote, we could pressure candidates to increase wages for women. It's scandalous. Women in factories today have it worse than I did sixty years ago when I worked in the Lowell textile mills."

Others joined the conversation as we cut or basted fabric:

"A woman doesn't have many choices to get pay for honest work."

"There's the sewing trades, or domestic service; about it for a woman on her own. Sewing pays starvation wages. In service, you get room and board, but you're paid a pittance."

"If you're educated, you can work as a nurse or teacher. Those are the best options."

"They pay a woman teacher less than a man."

"Women should be treated better at home. They work long hours and aren't paid at all. Many stay with a man who beats them 'cause they don't see how to feed themselves and their kids if they leave. It's gotta change."

This talk reminded me of library books I'd read, such as *The Man Who Laughs* by Victor Hugo, which explains causes of extreme poverty and the plight of the poor. At first I read fiction to pass evenings alone in my room, but I changed to non-fiction about nursing and social conditions. I became determined to find a way to earn money, because I did not want to spend my savings while in Malden, or to ask Frank or Katherine for spending money.

At Katherine's, I was up early to eat breakfast with Frank, the Parnell children, and the other boarder. Mrs. P. served porridge, toast, tea, and boiled eggs. She was pressed doing everything herself so I lent a hand with the carrying-out of dishes and made a good strong pot of tea.

Frank carried Katherine's tray upstairs before he left in the morning, and I placed pillows behind her and helped her sit up to eat. I poured her weak tea, even cut her toast if she felt tired. I supported her when she needed to get out of bed to use the toilet or tub. The purpose was to reduce strain on her body.

I encouraged her to change her position in bed frequently because I'd heard this would prevent bedsores. I sponge-bathed her on non-bath days, but encouraged her to wash her own face and brush her hair. "I don't want to turn you into an invalid when you're confined solely to prevent premature delivery of your baby."

After her morning nap I would often offer her a back rub. I'd gently rub tender areas, and those which appeared pressed, though I didn't know exactly what to look for. If Mrs. P. cooked mutton, I asked her for solidified fat; otherwise, I'd rub with castor oil, but had to buy the oil. I wondered if I were caring for Katherine properly.

She missed her sewing business, and getting out of the house. I accomplished our domestic duties in the morning, and ate lunch with her.

"Chutes and Ladders?" she might suggest after lunch.

Sometimes we played Old Maid. Both games were low stress. I preferred the card games. Fortunately, she hadn't adopted the superstition common among folks in Nova Scotia that cards were an agent of the devil.

One day she turned her pale face to me. "I hope all this lying flat on my back is worth it."

"The doctor thinks it provides the best chance for your baby to grow. A fully developed baby is likely to be healthier."

"I dreamt it wasn't right."

I noticed a tear form in the corner of her eye. "What do you mean, Kathy?"

"Instead of arms, he had wing-like things."

"Mothers always worry the baby'll have problems, but most come out perfect."

"I must try to picture a healthy boy."

"Be brave, Kathy." I patted her shoulder. "Now, I must run errands. If you don't sleep, have a look at one of these novels. They're cheery."

I skipped as I escaped the house.

"What do you think of teaching me to sew on your machine?" I asked one day. "I've seen them operated in houses where I boarded back home. I could learn quickly."

She hesitated. "Would you take great care with it, Del? Can I talk it over with Frank?"

"Of course." I thought she should be able to decide herself, since it was her machine. Frank and Katherine agreed I could learn to operate her Singer.

"Kathy, if I get good enough, I'll sew baby clothes for you. What do you think?"

She didn't answer, so I started hemming cotton baby blankets. My first seams wandered in unintended directions, but after they straightened I offered again, "Why don't we make some sleeping robes for the baby?"

"That'd be lovely, Del. I never should have doubted you'd learn the machine."

"You don't have to worry I'll take over your lingerie business. I like to learn new skills, but I don't have patience for fine sewing."

I enjoyed assisting Katherine and keeping notes for her doctor. By her sixth month of pregnancy, I could see an obvious bump in the blanket over Katherine's tummy.

Her doctor visited. "Miss Schwester, we'll have the delivery here in the home. I suggest, since you're obviously a reader, you learn about midwifery. Get hold of this book."

He scribbled on a scrap of paper: *Advice to Mothers* by Buchan, 1804.

*1804! Where am I likely to find that?* I understood by his hurried manner and superior tone it was my responsibility to figure out where the book might be obtained.

I asked him about the best way to prevent bedsores.

"Cleanliness, Miss Schwester, and stimulation of the skin by rubbing with mutton tallow or oil. Olive or castor may be the best. In houses where they don't get bedsores, they give a back rub, plus two sponge baths with gentle rubbing every day. And they move the patient every half hour. Just pulling the bottom sheet until the patient shifts pressure points may be enough. Katherine's thin, so check, especially, her bony areas like her shoulder blades and ankles. Pay attention to skin where the colour's unusual, or feels warmer or colder than the rest."

*I'll start a second sponge bath everyday, and a daily back rub. I'll move Kathy when she's sleeping.*

"I can see you're giving Katherine good care, but it wouldn't hurt to pay strict attention to the moving during daytime and evening. Her husband could shift her a bit whenever he gets up during the night."

"Thank you for your advice, Doctor."

As for Katherine, she welcomed the back rubs and the extra sponge bath.

I was well-known at the Malden Public Library by this time, so went there for Buchan's book. The librarian supplied me with a note of introduction to Miss Clarke, the head nurse at Malden Hospital, who agreed to lend me the volume. I devoured it.

A chapter on pregnancy care preceded the one on midwifery. Buchan disapproved of card playing during pregnancy because it caused fatigue. We stopped playing Old Maid.

After reading the chapter on midwifery, I concluded Buchan would have approved of how Mrs. Jung and I had delivered her baby, but not of the mother sitting in her rocker the next morning. The chapter also confirmed I was right in wanting to air the borning room after the delivery. Buchan recommended mothers have a midwife because doctors were too busy to attend properly to a delivery. I reflected that Katherine's doctor might expect me to support Katherine through most of her labour. His confidence in me strengthened my own.

I queried Katherine's doctor outside our rooms on his next visit. "Buchan's advice for pregnancy and delivery is for *ordinary* cases, but is Katherine's case *ordinary*?"

"Good question, Miss. It's not normal to spend months in bed, and some women become weak from it, so the effort of childbirth may prove too much. But we don't know how her delivery will progress. Rest assured, I'll have instruments in my bag, and use them only as last resort, as Buchan recommends. It's a matter of weighing risks."

# 11: Eyes twinkled

I returned Buchan's book to Miss Clarke. "Besides companionship, what responsibilities do you have for your cousin?" she inquired.

I mentioned my efforts to supplement the boarding house food for Katherine's and the baby's health.

"I ask because we'll be running a night course called 'Sick Room Cooking'. It's intended for our nurses in training, but I'm sure you'd find it useful."

"It would be."

"I can facilitate you being accepted. It starts next Tuesday and runs for six weeks. We're charging five dollars, plus a dollar for materials, but the school can cover the tuition if you can't find the money."

"Are there other costs?"

"We're using *The Boston Cooking School Cook Book* and you're expected to buy a copy. That's it. If you don't have a white apron, you may borrow one from our supply."

"Thank you for the opportunity. I'd like to enrol. And I can pay my way."

I smiled as I skipped back to Katherine's.

I attended the first class wearing my newly sewn white bib apron. Never a borrower nor a lender be, Mother always said.

We were only eight students. I met my partner, Deedee, a good-natured young woman, pretty in a broad, rosy cheeked way. "None of us at home spent time in the kitchen," she said. "We always had a cook."

I'd learned Mother's way of cooking. She produced three solid meals a day by estimating amounts or using the teacups and various spoons we had in the kitchen. At Malden's cooking classes, I learned to use standardized measuring cups and spoons to measure ingredients for recipes in the cook book.

The newer methods made sense to me and I adopted them easily, though Deedee's more casual attitude complicated our early efforts. She invariably overfilled our measuring instruments. "A little more'll make it better," she quipped.

Our first pudding set like lumpy, wet clay. Deedee gradually improved her concentration when measuring until our clear drinks, soups and gruels met with approval.

It surprised me, then, when our milk punch hit my throat with a burning effect. Deedee had decided to increase the recipe's one tablespoon of brandy. "Father would never accept a drink with a skimpy spoonful of brandy," she said as she winked at me and flashed her broad smile. I had to smile as well.

"You seem happy here at the hospital," I commented.

"Yes. It's damned hard work, but I feel useful."

"It looks as if you're well treated."

"Some supervisors think they have to be hard on you, but the head nurse is fair."

"That'd count for a lot."

"It does. Why're you asking?"

"Just interested, I guess."

"Nursing or teaching were my choices, or get married and have no independence. You'd find the studying a snap, though, Della."

"Well, I've tried teaching and don't really like it. Nursing might be better for me."

"I'm going to sneak a word by Miss Clarke about how super you are."

"Don't, Deedee."

"Oh?" Her eyebrows went up and her eyes twinkled.

On my way home in a cab, I wondered whether I'd miss the two remaining classes if Katherine went into labour.

# 12: Ordinary birth

Frank knocked on my door late the second Sunday evening in December. "Katherine was feeling her tummy muscles tighten once in a while, and now she's getting pains."

"How often?"

"About every forty-five minutes. I'm going out to call the doctor."

"Okay. I'm coming to sit with her. Tell Mrs. P. we'll need pots of boiling water."

I picked up the pile of linen I'd collected for the birth and went into Katherine's room. She appeared paler than usual, and perplexed with these new sensations in her body.

*Reassure her, be calm.*

I encouraged her to rest between her pains. As they became more intense, I wiped her brow and offered sips of water.

"If it's a boy, we'll call him Franklyn, Frankie for short, and a girl'll be Sarah. But I know he'll be a boy," Katherine said, and then dozed for a while.

Finally, Frank returned. "The doctor said to call him when the pains are every twenty minutes."

It was five AM before that happened, and six before the doctor arrived. Frank was off to work before the doctor encouraged Katherine to push.

I felt myself strain each time she did. In the end, she was pushing with every bit of strength she had. Her flesh tore when she pushed the head out. I wanted to cry for her when that happened. I did cry when we saw the baby.

The doctor held him up. "Mrs. Guibord, you have a perfect baby boy. Six and a half pounds, I'd say."

The afterbirth was expelled before the doctor washed up and prepared to leave.

Outside the room he turned to me. "It was an *ordinary* birth. Most are. Clean them up, and put the fellow to the breast as soon as feasible. Buchan recommends it. Call me if she has fever or excessive bleeding."

He left. I settled Katherine, who only wanted to rest, and I cleaned the room.

My whole body longed for a family. I wished for a husband, gentle like Frank, but more interesting than him. Katherine could look forward to motherhood. I had plans to discuss at Malden Hospital.

# 13: Nurse's aide

"We're interviewing now for student nurses," my instructress told me. "If you were approved, you'd probably start late summer. It depends when there's a student place free. Before you leave this evening, why don't you pass by the office and request the forms, and an appointment? I'm convinced you'd be an excellent nurse."

I had been able to attend the last two evening classes of 'Sick Room Cooking' and had handled the classes as well as anyone. Several students in the Malden School of Nursing talked positively of the training program there.

I returned to Katherine's in the highest of spirits. My main concern was financial. I'd already used savings to pay for the cooking course, for cabs to and from the hospital (for it wasn't wise for a woman to walk alone after dark in Malden), and for fabric to learn sewing on the Singer. My only income since arriving in Malden was the few dollars I'd earned sewing for ladies from Mrs. P's hospital support group. They'd wanted me to do more, but I didn't like to take advantage of Katherine's permission to use her machine, nor was I interested in sewing as a permanent occupation.

Katherine was regaining strength slowly. I washed clothes in the mornings, and minded Frank Junior while Katherine rested each afternoon. She would have been over-taxed to manage alone.

The time was approaching, however, when I should move on because Frank and Katherine would want their second room for a nursery. I didn't feel as confined as I did during her pregnancy, but I did long to be sociable with more people on a daily basis.

I was granted an interview, and was surprised to see both the head nurse, Miss Clarke, and the chief hospital administrator.

The administrator commented on my paperwork. "Miss Schwester, your forms are completed in an admirable script, have no unfilled spaces, and answer in correct grammar. Your letters of reference describe you as reliable, capable, and of good character. You were teaching school in Nova Scotia. Why are you considering a change of profession?"

"I'm more mature than when I began teaching. It was a job arranged by my family and initially I accepted it rather than embarrass my parents. I continued teaching for several years because it provided a means to earn a good salary and to live independently. When the opportunity arose to travel to Boston, I was attracted to the adventure. On reflection, I realized I enjoyed the personal nursing aspects of supporting my cousin, and that led to the idea of changing my profession."

"I pass you now on to our head nurse."

"Miss Schwester, what exactly were your nursing duties for your cousin?"

"I sponge bathed her, helped her manage eating while she lay in bed, arranged nutritious food to supplement the boardinghouse fare, encouraged her natural positive attitude, kept notes to report to her doctor, assisted him during the delivery, and helped Katherine establish nursing her infant."

"Have you other nursing experience?"

"Mostly of the first-aid sort that arose from accidents at school or in homes where I boarded as a teacher. I cleansed and bandaged cuts. In an emergency, I also acted as midwife in the birth of a healthy baby, without the guidance of a doctor. I've always gained great pleasure from helping people personally."

The head nurse looked at the administrator, who spoke. "We're concerned whether you have sufficient money to see your way through our program. The stipend we pay is tiny. You couldn't go travelling home to Nova Scotia on it, for example. Do you have paid work arranged for when you are no longer needed by your cousin?"

"Not yet. It was assumed I'd return to Nova Scotia, but if you accept me, I'll seek employment in Malden or Boston for the period until your next intake."

"I'll be frank, Miss Schwester. I have reservations about whether you could adjust to the status of a student nurse as you're used to being in charge of a classroom, and unused to following strict orders, or routines not of your design. We'll review your application and contact you by letter. It's been a pleasure talking with you."

*Are they testing how I react to their hesitation?*

"Thank you, sir, for hearing me, and thank you, Miss Clarke."

The head nurse smiled in an uninterpretable manner. Then she said, "Would you be interested in temporary employment as a nurse's aide? I warn you, it would involve lots of cleaning revolting messes and the pay is minimal. You could live, though, in our nurses' residence."

"That sounds wonderful." I accepted immediately and hurried back to Katherine's because I'd promised to style her hair.

"I want to surprise Frank." She held up a framed photograph. "He says this style's a 'killer' on me."

In the picture she wore her hair parted in the middle with a coiled braid pinned above each ear. I wore my own fine hair in its usual hurried bun.

I could not have been happy as she was, living in two rooms most of the day. It sent me stir-crazy when I minded the baby in the afternoon. And I could not marry a man who spent his day in a cage, like Frank in his elevator. True, he met lots of people, but what did he talk about with them? 'Floor?' 'Nice weather.' I needed more for my brain, more action, and more real interaction with people.

"Della, what did they say at the interview?"

"They didn't promise one way or the other." I shrugged. "But they're sending me a letter. I think they'll hire me as a nurse's aide in the meantime."

# 14: Nose to the grindstone

*Dear Miss Schwester,*
*We are pleased to offer you, immediately, work as a nurse's aide at the current rate of pay. Your formal one month probation will begin the fourth of August 1902, after which, if you prove yourself satisfactory to our executive committee, you may join regular nurse training. The probationary period is our normal procedure. You are required to respond in writing within one week, if you choose to accept this opportunity.*

Enclosed with this letter from the chief administrator was a list of what to expect at Malden Hospital nurse's training:

Provide your own uniform during probation
Expect to work long hours
Exemplary behaviour expected, similar to that of a teacher
Work in wards
Attend classes
One day a week off
Live in the nurse's residence attached to Malden Hospital
Meals provided in our residence dining room

I danced a jig when I saw meals were provided. My aide and probationary periods were more difficult than I'd imagined. I was a weakling compared to the experienced nurses and new intakes from farms. I fell into bed exhausted each night.

Bed making required perfection and speed. I was willing to comply with the expectation of perfection, but that coupled with speed eluded me. I saw myself as inept, clumsy, fumbling, for the first time in my life.

I didn't score well on the popularity front, either. Most probationary nurses were five years younger than me. They wanted a career in nursing, but their off-duty conversations revealed their number one goal: find a husband; and their number two goal: attend a party or 'walk out' with a young man.

Success at the nursing program was on my front hob, love and marriage floated somewhere in the back. I learned, when I enthusiastically launched into a monologue on our latest assigned chapter from Stoney's *Manual*, how disparate were our interests.

I failed a couple of initial chances to join the tribe-thinking of my colleagues. A classmate hatched the idea that those of us who had Sunday off should take the canal boat to Boston to enjoy an ocean voyage. I declined. "I've been on the ocean many times."

"Why don't you want to go, Della? We'll have a banger time together. Do you get sick on the water?"

I held onto my savings.

Deedee and I became friends, and there were a couple other women who had taught school. We teamed up from time to time for outings.

After a month of probation, Miss Clarke called me in for assessment. "Miss Schwester, how do you feel about your month here?"

"I've kept up with the reading and have worked as hard as I can. I don't always understand the reasons for requirements, but I try to comply."

"Yes, well, working hard and trying to understand are admirable qualities, but they don't necessarily produce the results required in our hospital. I've recorded that you are an average worker. You don't see into the work readily. It appears we agree, though we state the situation differently. How do you feel about our program? Do you wish to leave or struggle on with training?

"I definitely wish to continue."

"Good. I personally regard our work a vocation, a noble profession, though many call it a semi-profession or less. I think you share my opinion of the higher status, and I see in you the makings of a dedicated nurse, so I approve your acceptance into our regular program. Don't disappoint me."

She presented me the Malden School of Nursing student pin. "You may change your uniform at the end of this shift. Now return to your ward."

"Thank you, Miss Clarke!" I scurried off to change bedpans and cheer patients.

When news arrived about Mother's passing, I had to suppress my grieving, so I concentrated on improving the little skills like perfectly folded linens and swiftly made beds, those boring tasks my supervisors liked to inspect for flaws.

Each patient affected me differently. There was a man in his fifties whose employment had been in a glassworks. We were treating him with Fowler's solution for leukemia. As he reacted adversely to the first infusion, we slowed the second one.

I noted how he tensed his whole body when I approached with the needle and tubes. He didn't talk about fear for himself, though. "My wife's scrubbin' floors for money t' buy food. She has t' leave the kiddies with a neighbour all day."

"Try to relax yourself, sir. It'll help you get better. I'm sure it's what your good wife and children want." I tried to soothe him, but knew my attempt was inadequate.

I remember also a tonsillectomy patient, a quiet child whose parents had sent a tiny flowering cactus to cheer her. When I breezed into her room, she showed me hard grey liver cubes that she had kept from her lunch tray. "They hurt my throat," she said.

My jaw tightened. Of course she shouldn't eat hard food right after having her tonsils ripped out! What misguided kitchen worker had sent those overcooked cubes up? I poured a cup of cold water for the girl to sip, and sent an aide down to fetch applesauce and a milk pudding.

I frequently cared for post-appendectomy patients. One muscular man requested steak for his first meal. "Sorry, sir, the doctor ordered clear liquids. We'll see how you handle a broth and go from there."

I pretended not to hear his low volume curse words. He was reluctant to pull back his covers when I checked his incision for heat or oozing, signs of infection.

His discharge day arrived. "Continue with a bland diet, and no heavy lifting, or sports."

He groaned.

"Continue to check your incision and call your doctor if you notice anything unusual. Here's a list of most common complications. But you're doing well, so it's unlikely you'll have problems if you behave yourself. Good luck."

I smiled to see him walk arm in arm with his wife down the hallway.

I treasured my days off to walk in the quiet treed grounds of Malden Hospital, go on an outing with a friend to a garden, perhaps shop or visit Katherine.

One day I received a note from her.:

*This Sunday, when I believe you have a half day off, could you come for tea, as I would like to see you, and could you possibly care for Frankie for an hour or so? He's so active now he quite wears me down. I'd like to go out with Frank for a walk, just the two of us. Please be a dear and say 'Yes.' to me in a quick note.*
*Sincerely,*
*Katherine.*

She left almost immediately after I arrived. "Del, thank you for coming! Do you mind if I walk with Frank first? He'll go on to his stamp club meeting afterwards, and we can have tea together here."

She held her mouth muscles tightly, except for the involuntary tremble of her lower lip. She threw on her coat and the couple practically flew out the door.

Katherine should have mentioned Frankie was in foul humour due to a cold. He pulled at everything he could reach as he sped on all fours around the room, and he howled at the slightest frustration. The experience convinced me my future lay in nursing of adults rather than mind-numbing infant care.

Katherine smiled as she entered the room an hour later, carrying a small bag. "I've a treat to go with our tea. Let's go down to the parlour."

She handed the bag to me, scooped a few toy blocks into a sack, picked up Frankie with his rag doll, and we headed down the stairs. "If you'd occupy Frankie a few more minutes, I'll make the tea. I use the kitchen all the time now."

Frankie wailed, but she didn't turn around. I tried to entertain him with Patty Cake, The Farmer in the Dell and such songs until Katherine returned with a tea tray.

"These cannoli are the best. Thank goodness you agreed to visit. It gave me an excuse to buy them."

"You're looking well, Katherine."

"Thank you. I know I ran out shamelessly this morning. Sometimes I need to get away. Little Frankie's a pet, and I love him dearly, but I need a break now and then."

"Have you met any other parents?"

"Not really. I'm beginning to feel more energetic, though."

"Maybe if you joined a church…"

"Mrs. P.'s been trying to have us go to hers. Says there's a crêche, and visiting time after the service."

"You might meet other new mothers there, nice women."

Katherine laughed. "Yes, women who Frank would approve of!"

"Talking of the other kind, have you started sewing again?"

"Not yet, Del. I haven't felt up to it until recently."

"Maybe you could start with one client. See how you manage with a small project."

"I should. It's the only way we can save money. I was putting part of my earnings in a bank account before the baby."

"For anything special?"

"I want to buy a house."

"Ambitious!"

"Why couldn't I rent out rooms like Mrs. P.? I don't want to make meals like she does, but so many people come to the city every day, and they all need a place to stay. Most are good folks, like you and me."

"It's wonderful to see you returning to your old self. I've enjoyed visiting, but should be on my way to run a couple errands on my way back."

"But Del, I haven't heard about you. You're always running off."

We promised to get together before long, and did meet now and then, but study and work occupied the majority of my time.

The next spring, I passed the exams on Stoney's *Materia Medica for Nurses*, with all marks ninety per cent or higher. I felt confident to face another of Miss Clarke's reviews.

"You've improved. Your ward work's excellent of late," she told me.

I felt I could relax and reduce my study hours a bit so I could visit Katherine more often.

One time I accepted when a colleague invited me. "Del, come out on Saturday with me and my fellow. He has a friend visiting in town. It'll be jolly, the four of us."

We bought cold cuts and bread, strolled around Bell Rock Park, and had a picnic in the pleasant warmth. My colleague chatted easily, but the visiting fellow was as reserved as I was. I avoided other picnic outings.

Five months later, my marks from the Medical Board doctors were not so glowing, so I resumed a strict study schedule. By then I was immersed in the vortex of advanced ward work and study of Kimber's *Anatomy and Physiology for Nurses*. It seemed as though time was speeding up, and then my body rebelled.

A gentle discomfort in my abdomen, on the lower right side, increased in intensity over a couple of hours until my abdomen, though apparently flat, felt like it was protruding. I stood the pain as long as I could, and then sought advice from Matron.

She took my temperature. "How long have you had this pain?"

Our doctor prodded me, examined a drop of my blood under his microscope, and sent me to surgery for an appendectomy. I wanted to fight the ether as the mask came ever closer, and the nurse had to instruct me to "breathe deeply." Eventually I submitted to the gas.

It was December, 1904. I worried the time off for recovery would mean disastrous exam results. How would I catch up? I'd missed a whole month. And if I did pass the exams, would I find a job?

I pushed my nose to the grindstone from January onward to the final examinations in March.

Miss Clarke presented me with my nurse's pin. "Congratulations, Nurse Schwester, you graduate R. N. with an average of ninety-five per cent."

I grinned from my chin to my hairline.

She invited me to stay on at Malden Hospital as Night Supervisor. "You're grinning, Nurse Schwester. Most unusual for you."

So began a new period in Malden. My life was a routine of work, short outings on days off, and occasional visits with Katherine. I think the night supervisor role suited my personality, but it did nothing to encourage an expanded social life.

# 15: Applied to

Initially, I felt distanced from the upheaval when Canada followed Britain into war in 1914. President Wilson, and the majority of American people, preferred neutrality at the beginning of the war. They were already defending their southern border against sporadic threats from Mexico.

I grieved the loss of Father in spring. 1915. He had enjoyed life for ninety years. It was as though his passing increased disturbances in our family, country, and the world.

A letter from Charlene, dated June, 1915, brought the war closer to my heart.

> *I'm taking a few minutes, now the children are in bed, to write a note while my strawberry jam cools. Isn't the warm weather wonderful?*
>
> *I do hope you are recovering from the loss of your father. Take comfort in thoughts of his long happy life and remind yourself that he would want you to continue in your achievements. It must have been hard, though, to have missed his funeral. I think of you often.*
>
> *Our little Maud is a lively ten year old. I think we should have named her Anne Shirley instead of Maud, the author of Anne of Green Gables.*
>
> *Your brother, Dan, may not have informed you about our cousin, Geoffrey. He lined up to enlist first opportunity and promptly got his leg injured in France. He may have lied about his age. Geoffrey isn't much older than my youngest son. Last month the Huns sank the Lusitania, a Cunard liner. They say 128 Americans were aboard her, so maybe the States will join our effort. With them onside, we might get the War over soon.*
>
> *Pray I'll have cheerier news to share next letter.*
> *Sincerely,*
> *Charlene*

Geoffrey was lying in bed in a camp hospital. I wanted to help him.

Posters for the American Red Cross leaped out to rebel everywhere I went after Charlene's letter, but part of me wanted to continue in my hospital nursing. The posters gnawed at my gut. I wasn't doing enough to help young men like Geoffrey. The propaganda also flattered my need for a nobler role, and justified my yearning for travel.

I applied to join early in 1917. The United States declared war on Germany April 6, 1917.

~

"Halifax Swept by Flames After Explosion, 2000 Dead." This *Boston Globe* headline December 7 confirmed ghastly news I'd heard the previous day. A ship carrying explosives hit another ship in the narrowest part of Halifax Harbour.

My heart wanted to join the next trainload of doctors and nurses gathered to help the injured at home, but I was torn.

When I went up to relieve the day supervisor, she said in a sharp tone. "Della, it's a minute after the hour! I thought you'd run off to Nova Scotia. Look at you. Your apron's wrinkled and your hair's a mess."

I stiffened my spine and lifted my chin. "It's not in my work ethic to abandon my post."

She left in a huff. Afterwards, I sat and stared at nothing for a few minutes, before forcing myself to check the wards.

The headline had not exaggerated. People ran to watch the ships on fire and the rescue efforts. Then the ships blew up.

Charlene wrote that they had even felt the blast in East Cove:

> *You remember our niece from George's side of the family, the one who went off to Normal College in Truro? She was practice teaching on December 6th, and suddenly her desk and everything on it shook for no apparent reason; but if she thinks back, it was just after nine in the morning of the big explosion in Halifax, a hundred kilometres away! Doesn't it give you shivers?*
>
> *It's so sad, especially for the little orphans. Thank goodness some can be taken in by relatives in the country. They've got up now the Massachusetts-Halifax Relief Committee to handle the masses of money and things coming in, mostly from Canadians and Americans, and from kind people all over the world, too.*
>
> *Wish you were here, but I know you're helping out where you are.*
> *As ever,*
> *Charlene*

The Red Cross sent me to Camp Upton in New York State in February, 1918. It was like no other place I'd lived.

# 16: Camp Upton

Charge Nurse Almer, my immediate superior, welcomed me to Camp Upton with a rant. "Society ladies don't frequent our accommodation or hospital at Camp Upton. Fortunately, I might add, 'cause they breeze in with good intentions and disturb sensible routines of common workers."

I intended to get on well with Miss Almer. "I've done my share of bedpan cleaning, Miss Almer, and I agree with you."

"Miss Schwester, I see you've a teacher's diploma, experience as a floor supervisor, and you're close to the upper age limit for deployment to Europe. I'm assigning you a night supervisor position. Think you can handle it?"

"I do. What challenges have arisen in the past?"

"Our younger nurses get silly with so many men around. We must manage the girls with a short rein. We have authority to dismiss any nurse caught sneaking out in the evening. We can apply severe warnings, and must take quick action against insubordination. My advice to you is to not be lax with the nurses you supervise. Understand?"

"Yes, ma'am."

"There are two other matters, unfortunate ones. It's only right I tell you about them."

"I do want to be informed."

Miss Almer's voice dropped and she blinked several times. "Our patients are...different from the usual in a civilian hospital. Almost all of ours are men, many of them young, missing limbs, disfigured, or mentally damaged. You must try to maintain your composure when you meet them."

"I'll brace myself....There's another matter?"

"Yes, quite different. I'm going out on a limb to mention this, but it's only fair my nurses understand conditions that concern their safety. The military authorities have invited members of two rival New York street gangs to train here at Camp Upton."

I tensed.

"The brass think these fellows already know how to fight, and I agree on that point. The men have pledged a moratorium on their differences while in the army, but one never knows. Be alert to signs of friction, and don't put yourself in the crossfire should shooting erupt. All my nurses are aware of the situation and are asked not to discuss it."

"I understand. Thank you for your advice."

Nurse Almer dismissed me into the hands of a nurse who led a group of us around the Red Cross facilities. "We're a base hospital and have 120 nurses for 40 wards," she explained. "How many nurses for each ward? You do the math. We don't have private quarters for 120 nurses, so some of you will share a room. We expect a new building, but with luck you'll be into the action before it's constructed. From what I hear, our accommodation is a luxury resort compared to what you'll get across the water. Talking of water, we have hot and cold on tap, showers, and flush toilets. Don't count on such luxuries in France. Enjoy your time at Camp Upton, ladies."

I was to start duty that night, so I unpacked in my nun-like cell after the tour. Camp Upton felt unfriendly, with everything so square and un-adorned and the trees kept at bay on the outskirts. I thought it would be different once I got to know a few people, but knew it would not be easy to make friends, as a night supervisor. Would Camp Upton be like Malden hospital where the younger nurses' main interest was to get a husband?

Miss Almer was bang on about the struggle to appear calm when see-ing the damaged soldiers. Until Camp Upton, I'd nursed people who were sick from disease, or recovering from operations, but had seen few am-putees or faces disfigured from accidents. It took all my will-power to re-main calm when I entered a ward of men damaged by war.

I was less used to this branch of nursing than the ward nurses under me. "It'll get less hard," one said in an attempt to ease my shock.

I experienced a version of my East Cove blueberry nightmare after my first shift. Set in the trees surrounding Camp Upton, the figure chasing me was more shadowy, vaguely German, but somehow still the Deacon.

In my waking hours, I knew the frightening vision was only an expres-sion of my fears, and the shock of seeing so many war wounds. The sub-conscious fascinated me.

"Miss West regrets she can't come for duty tonight. She's ill," A col-league relayed the message immediately before my second shift.

"Thank you for telling me."

*I'll see the poor girl, if there's a quiet minute.*

I hurried to the nurses' residence as soon as my ward was settled. "Where's Miss West? I've come to look in on her."

"I don't know, Miss Schwester."

"Then who would?"

"I don't know."

"Don't be foolish. This is her room, isn't it?" I smelled heavy perfume.

"Yes, Miss, but I don't know where she's gone," said the nurse. She did not look at me.

"Tell me what you do know, or it won't be good on your record. I'll find out anyway."

The nurse hesitated before she spoke. "She went out with one of the New York fellows. He has a Chevy 490."

"She skipped her shift to go out with a fellow because he has a car!?"

"Yes, Miss."

"The next time you see her, tell her to come to me."

"Yes, Miss Schwester."

Miss West could provide no reasonable excuse for her behaviour, so I dismissed her from service. I felt relieved when Miss Almer backed my action. I also felt gloomy because I was once again distanced from most of my co-workers.

I helped with the practical tasks in the wards when necessary, wound dressing or urinal emptying. Some nights I would pass from bed to bed, attempting a word of cheer to any patient who was awake. We usually had enough nurses to care for physical wounds, but never enough to write letters for the patients, comfort them in their worries, or even serve sips of water immediately when requested.

Once, early on, I heard a man crying. "Is there something I can do?" I said.

"Nothing, Miss. I don't want my wife to see me with no legs. I'm use-less."

"Tomorrow you'll feel better. Many women continue to love their man." I knew my attempt to console him was inadequate.

Upton was but a sample of horrors I'd meet later. How would I cope in Europe?

My night shifts allowed me time during the day to visit our library in the Red Cross Nurse's Recreation building. There I could chat with women who enjoyed the activities I did, like reading. One book I leafed through was *Miss Billy-Married* by Eleanor Porter. It looked too tame for me.

"Have you read this one?" I asked a serious looking nurse who held a couple of thick volumes.

"Yes. It's light, but worth scanning through to the end. Miss Billy compares the adjustments necessary in marriage to those necessary in a clock."

I took her advice. The clock analogy set me reflecting. Would I be willing to adjust to someone else? And would I ever meet anyone interesting enough, someone who would put up with my need to do things properly, my restlessness?

I encountered the same nurse in the library another day. She looked stolid, like a washerwoman, but obviously she was a reader. I asked where she came from.

"A town out west."

"How do you find the camp?"

"I like it. The days are ordered. You?"

"It's okay here, but I'm looking forward to real war effort in Europe."

"There won't be much time for reading 'cross the water. May as well enjoy books here while we can."

"My name's Della Schwester."

"You can call me Madge. Is Schwester German?"

"The background is. I'm from Canada."

"The brass say we're to be called Sister, and by our first name."

"I like that idea. It'll eliminate a lot of problems for me."

"Did you hear the rumour? A man shot two people in the Camp, and he ran away. Everyone's upset about it."

"I won't worry too much until it's official. But thanks for telling me."

"See you again, Della."

Madge was a bit awkward in conversation, like me. I never learned her last name. Maybe it, too, was German.

*The Chicago Daily Tribune* reported the shooting incident in the paper's May 6, 1918 issue; our own *Trench and Camp*, May 13, 1918, said the murders took place in the pine barrens north of the infantry area. The tragedy may have been related to a gang feud.

I'd rather be in France, if I have to dodge bullets.

Miss Almer summoned me to her office in the afternoon, a few days after May 13. "Della, you must prepare to leave for Europe, without notice. The order has arrived."

"I'm ready, ma'am."

I felt like I had put my toe in a river and the current was pulling me in. I had to swim, for Geoffrey and all the young men like him.

# 17: Troopship, then

I shipped out from New York shortly afterwards, along with my medical colleagues and hundreds of youthful soldiers assembled for embarkation. One tiny cog in the great war machine. I vowed to see cousin Geoffrey in each wounded man.

Our troopship sported a camouflage job of white, light blue, brown, and dark blue. The pattern reminded me of a crazy quilt back in Nova Scotia.

I shared a tiny cabin with Karen, who was from Youngstown, Ohio, and two other nurses. Karen informed us, "It's the *Olympic*, built with a deck for luxury travel." The boat was fancier than I'd hoped for to take us across to England.

Frequent alerts for life jacket and fireboat drills reminded me of the danger waiting, and it showed up one day as a U-boat was sighted heading for us. Our captain ordered increased speed and we outran the menace. At the time, I didn't know details, but was relieved to sense our ship continue on her path.

The sea was calm, so only a few of my fellow nurses were bothered with seasickness. In the daytime, I liked to walk the decks, enjoy fresh air, and look at the water in hope of seeing a whale or dolphin. We were called to calisthenics daily, and I felt better after exercises.

We nurses worked several shifts in the ship's clinic. We conducted physical examinations of troops, administered treatment for venereal diseases, and cared for several cases of influenza.

"I could give you a good time on deck after dark. How about it?" older men, some of them toughened by service in the Border War with Mexico, would venture when no superior officer was within hearing.

The farm boys took opportunities to brush young nurses' chests, or to pat their derrières, 'by accident'. I kept my guard up all the time, and wished we were officers, like nurses in the Canadian forces, so the boys would not dare touch us.

"Oh God, another lecture," Karen complained one afternoon. "I'm brain dead from yesterday's on the nervous system. What's it this time?"

"Emergency surgery, then an update on military surgical equipment. I like them all, but the metric system and the French and German lessons make me feel like I'm back in grade ten."

The army band performed concerts and we were encouraged to attend them. In quiet times we read. I wrote to Katherine in Boston, and letters home to Charlene and to my brother Daniel.

I wondered why I missed my parents more and more as time passed, and especially on this crossing. I had wanted the adventure.

The days at sea flew by. Before I knew it we were on the Mersey River, not far from Liverpool. My roommates and I promised to keep in touch, but only Karen and I became friends.

I had to swallow my impatience when British officials boarded to check our papers and health status, once the *Olympic* lay tied to the pier.

Of course, all the nurses passed inspection!

We wore our best uniforms to disembark. I enjoyed my cape's warmth in the cool damp air.

We nurses gathered, as instructed, on the pier, where a lady volunteer, in a dark military-looking suit, said. "On behalf of King George, I welcome you to England." She then pointed to a vehicle. "Kindly board this motor tram, which will transport you to your residence."

I'd have to get used to the British accent,.

Amidst a week of orientation to British wartime life, I purchased items suggested necessary, such as a washbasin and a bar of soap; then I received my orders by letter from the Matron-in-Chief in London. It began with standard army wording, which struck me as strange at the time:

> *I am directed to request that...*

Later I became used to the British Army style of expression.

When I boarded the train to the Salisbury Plain, I knew my European adventure had really begun.

# 18: Orientation

I arrived at Fargo Hospital late in June, 1918 by train from Liverpool and handed Matron my letter.

Matron welcomed the newly arrived personnel. Then she told those of us from the American Red Cross, "Unfortunately, I haven't been informed whether you're entitled to claim pay and allowances from the Southern Command Paymaster, as are the regular Q.A.s stationed here." The Q.A.s were members of Queen Alexandra's Imperial Military Nursing Service.

I bristled against the confusion, though I should have been used to it, after months treading water at Camp Upton in New York.

Matron continued, "Our hospital was built to care for 1200 patients, 36 to a ward, but lately we've crammed extra cots into the wards on a daily basis. Your dormitory is in the two-storey building you may have noticed when you arrived. Prepare yourselves for demanding shifts, starting tomorrow. Today, I want you to become familiar with our facilities."

She introduced a volunteer guide, Janice, a wizened woman who exuded energy and spoke with an upper class English accent. I was disappointed not to plunge immediately into saving lives, and at the same time relieved, because the British nurses at Fargo looked thin, weary, and overwhelmed.

Janice wasted no time. "Come, my dears," she addressed me and three Americans who had arrived on the same train from Liverpool. "We'll catch a lorry to the canteen. I expect you need a cuppa."

I appreciated tea. My American colleagues' shoulders slumped, though they smiled. They had been hoping for a good coffee.

The lorry, a Maudslay, looked like a tractor with a flatbed attached to the back. Our guide pulled herself up to the passenger seat while I and the three other new Q.A. Reserve nurses climbed onto the flatbed with me. Fortunately, it had sideboards installed. Four turns of the crank and the marvellous petrol engine chuffed awake.

The driver shifted it into gear and we toured around the various military camps. I saw endless rusting corrugated iron huts and larger buildings. Even the church and cinema were constructed of corrugated iron. Fargo looked like a bigger version of Camp Upton, except the huts were metal, less friendly-looking.

I yelled through the canvas divider to our guide. "Are these buildings dormitories?"

"Yes, they accommodate soldiers who train here, often for more than a year. Sick and wounded military personnel are treated in the buildings fitted out as hospitals."

"There must be thousands of people."

"More like hundreds of thousands. We have personnel from all over the Empire, resistance fighters from invaded countries, and now you Americans."

I didn't correct her. It was always awkward. I didn't want to make an issue about being Canadian because I *was* deployed with Americans, and they were so proud of being American.

"Here we are," our guide said.

I saw a shed that would look shabby on a modest American farm. "The Colonel Bogey March" blared out the doorway as a soldier exited. It was three o'clock in the afternoon. Another soldier came out. They waved gaily, bowed in our direction, and continued on their way, at the same time belting out lines from the popular song.

"Shall we go in, Sisters?" Janice asked. I heard in her tone a polite command.

We were the only female customers in the canteen, and the soldiers who made way for us to approach the counter sized us up. I hadn't yet become used to so much attention. The younger nurses blanched. Then we exchanged a look, with raised eyebrows, straightened our shoulders, and led by our guide, walked the gauntlet.

She crisply ordered for us. "If you would be so kind, five teas and five cream scones, with jam."

The music didn't stop, but in my ears there was silence. We carried our lunch to a long table where we managed a few bites before being interrupted.

"Mind if I sit here, Sister?"

"When you're finished, would you chat with me?"

"I was going to ask that one."

"Give the Sisters a few quiet minutes, gentlemen, before you crowd them," Janice said.

Tea enjoyed, I visited with boys who could have been my sons, and aging soldiers who could have been my father, and I took care to accept no future obligations. The soldiers showed off as if this were their last opportunity to impress a woman. I tried not to imagine these men wounded.

Once more, Janice directed us. "I've gotten us a ride back. Come, it's near dinner time."

"Have dinner here with me," one man pleaded.

"I can get us a ride to Amesbury. There's a real restaurant there," a bolder one offered.

*Some chance. Go off to Amesbury with one of these fellows.*

Janice had conjured up another chauffeured Maudslay. We climbed on board, literally, as the flatbed's base was wood, and returned to the military hospital for our meal.

The menu read "bangers and mash, spotted dick". Janice translated. "Dinner's sausages with mashed potatoes and dessert. Now, I must be off home. Matron's asked a staff nurse to show you the ropes over in the nurses' dorm after dinner."

Janice didn't explain spotted dick, and I noticed giggles from the nurses near us in line. I asked a friendly looking face. "What's so funny?"

"We always leave that for the Americans to find out."

More giggles, and one snort from a woman named Bonnie who said, "Try it, you'll like it," and burst into ribald laughter.

Food was food, so I tried the dessert. It was a steamed pudding with currants and custard sauce. Sweet and milky, it felt good in my stomach after the greasy sausages.

A history teacher turned nurse explained across the dining table, "A chef, Alexis Soyer, invented spotted dick about seventy years ago. He also invented a field stove for the British Army."

I thought she might become a friend. She was the staff nurse assigned to show us our dormitory.

We collected our bags from storage at Reception and followed her to our building, and up wooden stairs. There were forty cots in my room, a small table and, surprise, a washbasin beside each one. My appointed cot was next to the nurse who had been in line downstairs, the woman called Bonnie.

She sneered. "I s'pose you don't think much of this 'otel, since you're from 'merica where everything's posher."

There's always one.

"Oh no, it's lovely to have a clean bed," I replied. I had thought the British would be glad to have nurses, would not be hanging onto old resentments. I wanted to write home about conditions and my feelings.

*But if I write to Dan, the staff will see the name Schwester and know it's German. Bonnie will be even nastier. What can I write about? Can't describe the camp, or food, truthfully, 'cause the censor will black it out.*

*England,*

*June 27, 1918*
*Dear Katherine,*
*How warm is early summer this year? Is Frankie still interested in going along on your Sunday strolls in the park? He felt too grown up for a hug from me the last time I saw him. It made me a bit sad. He's an intelligent, good looking lad, though. Will be a hit with the girls.*

*I have finished a day of orientation, which included a tour of sur-rounding land and facilities. When I asked where the toilets were at one place, the worker looked blank, and then said, "You mean the 'water closet'?" They also call it the 'loo'.*

*They've put me in the Queen Alexandra Imperial Military Nursing Service as a Reserve member - and tell me membership indicates a high level of nursing training and character. I'm to sign the letters Q.A.I.M.N.S.R. after my name on official documents. Informally, they call us QAs, which is less of a mouthful, isn't it?*

*Could I bother you to let my brother, Dan, know I've arrived safely to my posting?*

*May you make progress in your ambitions to save for a house, and most important, may you, and all your family keep well,*
Yours sincerely,
Della

# 19: Check on a chap

"Wake up, Sister. It's five o'clock!"

The maid passed by my cot. I heard her only faintly, and checked my watch. I'd asked for five AM wake-up, but it was already well past the hour so I splashed water on my face, threw my uniform on and ran down steps, and then over to the dining room.

Several nurses were finishing breakfast. I downed my fried eggs and fried bread too fast to register the greasiness, and welcomed the cup of tea. We were allowed a small amount of milk in it.

"Today's yer lucky day, Sister. The milk's not watered."

"Super."

"Yer new 'ere, ain't yer?"

"Yes, first day on the wards."

"God bless yer. We need the 'mericans."

"Thank you."

"Sister Della?" A friendly voice. She sat down, a British QA younger than me. I noted her thin face, the dark circles under her eyes, her chalky front teeth. I recognized her uniform, similar to mine.

"Yes, Sister," I replied.

"Good morning. I'm Sister Emily. Most call me Sister Em. You're to work with me today."

"It's nice to meet you."

"Our ward's over-full, was built for thirty-six cots, but we're cramming extra in. I fear the twelve hours'll be hard on you."

"I'm here to work."

"Good attitude. Time we head up."

We walked side by side up the wooden stairs. "The brass have hired ward maids for less skilled jobs. It's a money-saving ploy."

"A maid came by with a wake-up call. What else do they do?"

"Deliver patients' meals, change beds, less skilled work."

"Don't they miss worrisome signs we'd note while doing routine tasks?"

"Yes, they miss a lot. We'll talk about it later. Here we are at our ward."

"It *is* really full!" An olfactory cocktail of Lysol, sodium hypochlorite, and strong soaps blasted my nose.

"First, we get the night sister's update."

Sister Frances, skinny like Sister Em and more exhausted looking, reported a regular night shift. Patient D continued to pull off his bandages, saying he wanted to die. Six other men had passed during the night. Five of them were influenza patients. All six bodies had been sent to the morgue. Eight patients from more crowded wards had taken their places. Large sterile bandages had been ordered again, but none had arrived. Lysol bottles should be saved for re-use as they were in short supply.

"If no staff nurses show up, the two of you'll have to carry on the best you can, with the ward maids, as we did last night. Good luck, sisters." She sighed. "I'm straight off to bed."

Sister Em said she'd check on the bandage situation and would begin changing the smaller dressings most in need of re-doing. She directed me to the corner of the room where the flu patients were situated. "Check their needs and do what you can for them. Wash your hands well afterwards."

"Sister Em, do we have masks?"

"We don't bother with them."

*Get on with it, Della.*

"Ask if there's something you need."

"Thank you, Sister."

I protected myself by not breathing close to a patient's face, cleansing my hands and nostrils with disinfectant solution, and washing my clothing as frequently as feasible. There was no time to wash hands between patients. Most required care for battle wounds as well as influenza. The men breathed with difficulty, having fluid or mucus on their lungs.

"Sister Em, do we use oxygen to help their breathing?"

"We don't have the equipment here. The men do as well without it."

I noted my patients' most immediate needs. One soldier had died during our updating by Sister Frances. The corpse was sent to the holding room for official death certification.

I completed a tour of re-positioning the men in bed, and was appalled at the stained linens. All patients needed hydration, so I asked my ward maid, Miss Bucks, to fetch water.

"Yes, Sister, but it's near breakfast time, and the men haven't eaten since four-thirty tea yesterday."

"Very well. Serve them breakfast. And bring along water as soon as you can afterwards."

"Yes, Sister."

Changing beds had to wait because Miss Bucks delivered the breakfast of tea, toast, and oatmeal gruel. I ensured the patients who had one or two arms and hands could reach their food. Then I cycled between feeding a man who had no arms and assisting others who were especially weak.

It took time to put the right amount on a spoon, and to position the spoon gently in the patient's mouth so he could work his muscles efficiently for swallowing. I tried to allow patients to swallow food completely before I offered more. I smiled at an improbable blessing: the lukewarm temperature of the food saved time because I didn't worry about burning a patient's mouth.

Miss Bucks fed patients also. I observed she needed training, but when could we find time?

"Miss Bucks, kindly help patients sip water while I re-bandage wounds."

Our supply of small sterile pads was adequate. I also delegated bed changing to Miss Bucks while I administered morphine to patients suffering severe pain. Many men who'd been given a leg amputation by the brutal guillotine method required morphine.

Patients with minor pain received aspirin. I wished I could do more to reduce the men's suffering.

My corner of the ward calmed after the patients were fed and medicated. Sister Em stepped smartly among her cots. Our day was flying by.

"Take a cuppa yourself when the meal comes up for patients," she called to me.

But she didn't take a break herself, so I didn't, either. Sister Em also worked with a ward maid, a willing person untrained in nursing, like Miss Bucks.

By four-thirty afternoon tea, all our patients had washed faces and clean sheets. Three more bodies had been sent to the morgue, and three new patients had soon arrived.

I'd re-bandaged mangled arms and leg stumps. The laboured breathing and coughing of my influenza patients would alert anyone to sickness in the room. I wiped mucus, and cooled fevered brows.

"Feels good, Sister."

After tea, Miss Bucks gave sponge baths and back rubs and re-offered sips of water. I distributed drugs and changed dressings.

It was a little less busy than the morning, so we could spend a few minutes chatting with the men. Sometimes I thought friendly talk and a gentle touch were the best medicines in our arsenal.

Patients without influenza smoked. Between puffs, one chap, Sam, liked to make plans. "Me and the missus are starting a shop when I get outta here."

"I got an idea meself," spoke up Alvin.

"What?"

"Gonna be a stump remover."

"Cut it. Not funny," Sam retorted.

"Don't get yerself in a flap, Sam."

"What've you got in mind?" I asked Sam.

"The missus is a cracker sewer. She can sew at home, classy stuff. I can order yardage straight from a mill. See? Got contacts. Make a profit on the fabric."

"You're starting small."

"Right, Sister. Won't have to borrow."

"Good."

"When it gets busy, we'll open a shop. I'll keep on with ordering, and tend the counter. Don't need legs to run the till."

"Hey, you've given me an idea," Alvin piped up.

"Better be good," Sam said.

"My girl makes the best fudge ever."

"Everyone loves a sweet," I said.

"Right. And she wraps parcels somethin' beautiful. Her father was a designer, you see, in one of them mills Sam was talking 'bout."

"Yeah," Sam said. "She could sell her fudge door to door, build up interest. Then the two of you could set up a stall, go bigger. Eventually rent a shop next to mine."

"Good luck with your plans, gentlemen. Excuse me, I should check on a chap over there."

The man I went to was crying. "Hello there." I attempted a soft tone, a friendly smile, not too broad or open.

"Sorry, Sister. Couldn't keep it away."

"No need. Can I pass a minute with you?"

"Yes." Sniff.

"Anything I can do?"

"No, Sister. They killed my younger brother. Why him?"

"I'm sorry. We can't know the why."

"Feel so lonely. We were best friends."

"Maybe when you get better, you can do something in his memory."

"Maybe. But I feel so lonely."

"Can I get a damp cloth for your face?"

"Thank you, Sister."

I fetched a washcloth and a glass of water for him, then touched his shoulder. As I went on to other demands, he thanked me again.

I felt inadequate to deal with the men's deep losses.

At six PM two QAs relieved Sister Em and myself.

"We must report four deaths, including the one which occurred during our briefing by Sister Frances," Sister Em said. "There are four new patients, all flu cases. And there's a skimpy supply of drugs in reserve. More have been ordered."

We scrubbed up and headed to the dining room for tea and supper. I'd learned to make do with plainer and fewer supplies than I was used to in the States. It was the British way, along with the words 'cuppa' and 'flap'. After a few weeks, I was feeling well introduced to their culture.

We received daily mail service and whenever possible, I went over to Reception in hopes of getting news from home as soon as it arrived. More often than not, I was disappointed.

# 20: At Stonehenge

The nurses were all atwitter because they'd seen me talking with Charlie at Reception when he delivered our mail. "Sister Della, whatever did you find to talk about with the postman for twenty minutes?"

"Oh, this and that. His accent sounded familiar, so I asked him where he came from."

"And...?"

"I think he's from...close to my home in Nova Scotia."

"Doesn't take twenty minutes to say that."

"He's awfully nice. His name's Charlie and he's going to come for me next Tuesday, my day off. He works extra and his officer lets him choose his leave, as long as the mail gets delivered."

"What if your day off is cancelled?"

"Don't you girls worry about that. He comes by daily, so it'll be easy enough to get a message to him." I was concerned, though, about Matron's sharp eye.

Tuesday, no Charlie at the agreed time. Humiliated, I hid my nose behind a book in a waiting room, and hoped Matron or Bonnie didn't walk by.

Charlie, all flustered and full of apologies, showed up an hour late. "So sorry, Della, the barracks cat threw up in my boots, and when I went for my 'cycle, it had a flat."

The bike was a well used Raleigh. Oh how I wanted a bike! No plodding along with vehicles zooming past. No waiting for some noisy, smelly petrol machine with a conceited driver. I'd just hop on and cruise at my own speed wherever I wanted. I'd feel the air rush by, hear the birds, smell flowers or trees, whatever was blooming. I'd feel twenty years younger if I had my own bike.

"Hop on the crossbar," he said.

"With this skirt?"

"Hitch it up and keep it out of the works. We'll be fine."

"Where are we going?"

"You deserve a real tour, Sister Della. I'm taking you on my delivery route."

"I don't want to get you in trouble."

"Captain won't mind. It's my bike."

"Bikes are in short supply. How did you get this one?"

He stood taller and breathed deeply. "I was first to volunteer to deliver mail. Then I convinced the captain that a 'cycle would help me train to be a dispatcher. He wouldn't apply for funds, but he signed permission for me to buy a bike. Canadians are paid better than most of the others."

"I see you've shined it up."

"Yeah, but the tires are half-covered with chalk dust already. Better than muck from rain."

I climbed on the crossbar and we cycled to The Parkway, a main road. We headed toward West Down South Camp.

On the way we visited Stonehenge. Can you imagine? Stonehenge! I had never dreamed of getting there!

The mysterious rocks were surely not a natural part of the landscape. I dismounted and ran around like an excited child, from one bluestone monolith to the next. A few of them were propped up with timbers and gave an idea what the place had looked like in prehistoric times. I hoped someone would put the structure together again in future.

The site radiated a power sensed by ancient people. I felt the strength of faith it would take to move such boulders and arrange them in a meaningful way, though I couldn't figure out their purpose.

We should have biked on, but we prolonged our time at Stonehenge. We sat on the dry grass.

"Do you have any brothers or sisters?" Charlie asked.

"Nine living. There were twins, but they died as babies. What about you?"

"I have an older sister. She raised me in Little Bland after my mother died."

"I'm sorry."

"It was a long time ago. Where did you grow up?"

"East Cove."

"Really! I was born close to East Cove, but don't remember anything about it. What's it like to have so many brothers and sisters?"

"We didn't have a lot of money, so we slaved to feed and dress everyone."

"What do you miss from home?"

"Besides the people? A good dinner of sauerkraut and Lunenburg sausage. We'd be really popular if we said that to others around here right now, wouldn't we? With my surname, I can't joke about missing kraut."

We laughed and laughed at this joke.

"I could do with a homemade blueberry pie," Charlie said. "Actually, anything from the fishing village." He changed to a wistful tone. "I was in such a hurry to get away. I even miss the smell from cod flakes!"

"Will you go back after the war?"

"I will. My uncle promised me the house. I've got plans, Sister. I'm saving money to buy a boat. It'll be called The Mink Fisher. I'll hire a couple of helpers and take over my uncle's herring grounds. There's a good living in fishing, along with farming and a woodlot. You can do all that in Nova Scotia."

"I plan to go back, too, eventually." A smile overtook my face.

"There should be work for nurses after the war," he said and then dug into his canvas bag. "No pie, but I saved bread and bacon at the mess this morning. Like a sandwich?"

"Bacon! I haven't seen it in our dining room yet. How thoughtful."

We leant against rocks warmed by the sun while we munched and chatted. So quickly, we became more than casual friends. I noticed he had a dark reddish oval mark on the inside of his right wrist, but didn't ask him about it.

"Time for letter delivery," he said. "Hold on, we've miles to cover."

I could see, as we passed close by on the bicycle, a lot of deterioration of the sheds. Mostly, the tin buildings had few soldiers present. I guessed they were on exercise.

The guards were normal, strong people with four limbs each. After wards filled with sickness and mutilated bodies in Fargo Hospital, it was uplifting to see healthy people.

Charlie stopped here and there to deliver letters. Guards grinned with pleasure when they received packets for their building.

I suspected Charlie had devised an abbreviated route for us, and my bottom was relieved when he said. "Enough work. Let's stop for a cuppa at the Canteen."

"Right on."

We returned, after tea, to Fargo Hospital. I tripped a mini jig before skipping up the stairs toward a sobering interrogation.

# 21: Rules are

Three young nurses full of questions greeted me at Reception. I opened my mouth, but was interrupted by one of them. "Sister Della, hm-m-m, a little word on the side. Matron is in a tear. She ordered me to send you to her on your return. Be suitably contrite."

Off to Matron I marched.

"Sister Della, I see you have returned." Matron's eyes had deep dark circles.

"Yes, Matron."

"Did you have a pleasant outing with your Private friend?"

"Yes Matron. He gave me a tour to—"

"I don't have to hear the sordid details, or a concocted story. You know the rules, Sister. You are not to fraternize with common soldiers. You are, at all times, to uphold the superior reputation of Queen Alexandra nurses. I'm disappointed in your blatant disregard for the conditions of your employment here."

"Matron, Private Rafuse was born in the same town as I was. He may be a relative. We just visited and shared news."

"I don't care what you shared, Sister. Rules are to be respected. You're on probation. One more infraction and you'll be dismissed with a dishonourable discharge. Do you understand?"

"Yes, Matron. I'm sorry to have caused you—"

"No need to blather. Get on with you."

"Yes, Matron."

I smelled chlorine in the fake ham that starred on our menu that night, and had been featured every leave day since my arrival. Was imitation ham the Fates' punishment for my day off?

I swallowed a slab of salty meat, and ate mashed potatoes and canned peas, then dragged myself to my dorm where I wrote a self-censored note to Charlie.

*England*
*July, 1918*
*Dear Charlie,*
*Today was perfect at Stonehenge, the whole tour with you, actually. Perhaps, because we both come from the South Shore, it's easy to talk with you. No, it's more than that. I've met others from home and found chatting awkward. You don't talk at me, you listen, con-*

*tribute, and talk with me. That's the art of conversation, isn't it? To value the other and add to the 'soup' of exchange.*

*I'm envious of your bike, but you probably guessed that. It's unfortunate, indeed, that our church considers envy a sin. I plan to get a cycle of my own as soon as possible. It will have red trim like yours. And I'll buy a divided skirt to go with it. Won't we make a picture on the roads of Nova Scotia! Come to think of it, I'll need at least two cycling outfits, because of the dust. Do you think the government will ever apply asphalt on the back roads?*

*I knew the rules here, but didn't think Matron would get upset about me visiting, on my day off, with someone who is practically a neighbour from the other side of the Atlantic. In fact she definitely laid down the law when I returned in the afternoon. She finished by telling me. "… if you fraternize with this soldier again, or in any other manner go against our rules, you will be discharged."*

*Since it's clear we must not see each other again as long as one of us is in military service, you must promise to correspond with me. We have so much in common. I've figured out we may be fifth cousins through my Great Aunt's second marriage to a Rafuse in Halifax. They settled eventually in Los Angeles. Amazing, isn't it?*

*Do be assured that I wish to continue our friendship, and since letters are the only means possible at this time, I eagerly await a note from you.*
*Sincerely,*
*Sister Della (Della to you)*

Laundry still had to be faced, as there wasn't time to wash clothes on a workday. The nurses' wash house contained many tubs where we could scrub clothes and linen by hand. We provided our own washboard, and bought soap at the commissary.

I hated the dark, crowded space where some nurses went out of their way to exchange crude jokes. My uncle's fish shack was more restful and smelled better than the wash house, with its damp air stinking of dirty laundry, harsh soap, and human sweat. At least in the wash house we had clean water.

In our enormous drying room, we spread wet laundry over poles which we then raised by cords, much as blinds were operated. The clothes dried naturally in sunny weather, but, usually, I had to gather my clean items while they were damp and iron them dry.

This night I hung my laundry and walked directly to my dorm. I opened my diary to write a few lines and fell into a dream. Bonnie stood behind and to the side of young nurses who gleefully saw me off on my outing with Charlie. Next, Bonnie was alone, beside Matron's internal mail slot. A long slim hand posted an envelope.

It was dusk with a clear sky. I raced over a charred, smokey field. An Alsatian dog was barking, and human guttural syllables became more and more distinct. I flattened myself into a depression in the field and smeared as much charcoal as I could over myself. Suddenly, a dark cloud appeared and a lightning bolt burst forth. The dogs became unnerved; the soldiers turned back. My mind repeated the sequence until dawn.

The next day, I nursed in an amputation recovery ward, and later assisted in surgery. I faced the work with determination, like we at home would face a gale at sea.

*England*
*July 2018*
*Dear Della,*
*I'm deeply sorry to have caused you trouble, but unrepentant about our outing because I swear you are the love of my life. Never did I think I'd fall so suddenly, and for a woman like you. It's your school mar'm way that has shattered my resistance, as if your being the opposite of me, completes me. We were comfortable together and shared experiences and jokes as only two souls from the South Shore could. I pray some day you may feel as I do.*

*Be assured, I'll not endanger your reputation with Matron, and be equally assured we'll find a way to know one another better.*

*Yes, we must continue to exchange letters. I have no control over how long I'll be delivering mail to your hospital, so letters may arrive irregularly, as is common these days. I beg your patience.*
*Sincerely,*
*Your Charlie*

# 22: A response

*England*
*July 1918*
*Dear Charlie,*
*Am I developing a strange awareness? A crow pecked carrion and I sensed I was the crow. My feeling was spontaneous, just was. Happened. That was at Camp Upton, New York State, some months ago.*

*Here in England, I've felt the pain of an injured worm, and the helplessness of other worms lost on dry walkways. I even sense the happiness of healthy plants, and the terror of trees that have limbs pruned, or lose roots at construction sites. I hear a dead cat call silently, as an amputated finger would. I see rocks, the least conscious entities of Nature, creating memories of events around them, and I record my own.*

*No matter how I try, I cannot achieve this sense of oneness with certain human beings. It's easier with loved ones such as family, or with you, but with Bonnie? Or a German?*

*Don't fear I have been too long on a Ouija board. I simply try to understand what is real to me. If the brass send me to France, I may have to nurse German prisoners, possibly the person who wounded my nephew, Geoffrey. Can I be one with that soldier?*

*Ignore my rhetorical questions, but write a line when you can, and no matter where or when you're sent, take care to come back. You are me.*
*Sincerely,*
*Della*

Matron added surgical assistance to my training. I had the opportunity to review the set up and operation of a Carrel-Dakin drip. American run CCSs (Casualty Clearing Stations) used the expensive, American-produced drip. I was trained in pre-operative blood transfusions, which were frequently necessary because patients arriving at a CCS often had lost so much blood the men needed replenishment prior to an operation.

Shifts of actual surgical assistance reminded me how demanding the male doctors could be. I thrived on keeping tools in order so I could present the correct one instantly, comprehending terms not heard since training, sharing the elation when we saved a limb or rescued a young man whose body flirted with death's invitation.

News from Charlie didn't arrive. My letters to him seemed superficial when I re-read them, because there was so much I couldn't write because of censoring. As I'd known Charlie for such a short time, I minimized, in letters, the extent of my growing affection for him. It was new to me, this feeling of attachment.

I concluded Charlie was in France, so wrote yet again.

> *England*
> *July 1918*
> *Dear Charlie,*
> *Are you well and doing the work you wanted? I pray so. It's exciting work, and beneficial to our cause, but do take care as best you can.*
>
> *After a week of fine weather, thunderstorms started. I went with three other QAs to town for lunch the last time I had a break. We enjoyed the soup, mulligatawny, they called it, and plaice (fresh fish!), with boiled potatoes and carrots and peas, the latter canned, of course. A lady pianist played soft, gentle music at the restaurant, and the atmosphere was friendly, a 'We're all in this together.' feeling. It seemed a world away from the hospital. We'd planned shopping after lunch, but the rain wouldn't stop, so we took the first chance back to the hospital on an open-backed lorry, and arrived happy, if drenched, with hours of daylight to spare. The QAs were good sorts, but the outing would have been more fun if you and your sense of humour had been with me.*
>
> *I've been given a wide range of experience, some of it intense, in preparation for later. It's difficult to maintain a properly humble attitude, when I'm used to supervising, but I try my best to learn new ways - never know when it'll be necessary to use any one particular skill. I feel alive, on the cusp of participating fully in our cause.*
>
> *Write a short note so I know you are O.K.*
> *Miss our chats at mail delivery time,*
> Sincerely,
> *Della.*

At long last I got a response!

*France*
*July 1918*
*Dear Della,*
*I hope you are keeping well.*
*The work is what I wanted, and it promises as much excitement as I can handle.*
*The memory of talking with you, and being with you, continues to warm my heart. Your recent letter arrived, and it so lifted my spirits. We will find a way to visit. I love you.*
*Sincerely,*
*Charlie*

In mid July, Matron recommended I maintain myself in a constant state of preparedness for re-posting. Orders often arrived with less than a day's notice. "You'll join a surgical team. With luck, you'll be with another nurse and an orderly."

My orders arrived very soon after that conversation.

I was transported from Fargo by truck and train to Folkestone. We QAs were herded onto the train at Amesbury and Pancras stations. On the train, we were assigned seats, and then the transfer to our ship at the port was, again, a mass of people, hurry, hurry, wait, wait.

Most of the trip was in darkness, and it was impossible to access a sanitary facility when I needed one for relief. Fortunately, our crossing was smooth, without enemy attack. Amidst army-style haste and delay, we disembarked in Calais, and boarded a train, direction unknown.

Marie Mossman

# 23: The river

The brass sent me to a CCS behind the front, close to the River Marne. I triaged and assisted our surgeon as needed. The other nurse administered and monitored anaesthetics until she fell sick, and then I took over her nursing duties.

Our orderly acted as a general helper. He moved patients, changed beds, washed men, even changed dressings when we were overwhelmed with hours and hours of constant operations.

The wounded men, boys really, kept coming. We operated on those who might live, and comforted the hopeless cases as best we could. We couldn't always stem the bleeding. Men called out to their mothers or sweethearts.

Nephew Geoffrey's image flashed through my mind. I told myself not to cry, to focus on work.

Early on, we were cut off from food supplies and used up our canned reserves. There were stories of eating rats. I wondered if we would ever be so desperate. Lots of rats thrived in the trenches and fields where they feasted on the wounded and dead.

A couple of able men risked their lives to forage at night and once came back with a dog. "Can you cook up a meal with this beauty, Sister?"

"We don't eat dog," I said.

"Come on, Miss. Them fellas're weak enough already. The dog's already shot."

"I've never cooked a dog."

"You cook it or our patients starve. What about it?"

I clenched my teeth. "Okay."

The dog was covered with muck, but underneath had blackish grey, woolly fur. Its powerful bone structure would support eighty pounds or more of muscle if it had been well fed. Its ears had been clipped, and its tail docked.

I asked what kind it was.

"Probably a farm dog gone stray," one of the hunters said. "It came right up to us when beckoned. Looks grimy now, but the meat underneath'll be fine. You'll see after I skin it."

He whipped out his pocket knife and carefully cleaned it with one swipe on his trousers.

Another of the men volunteered to cut up the meat. "I'm the butcher back home in Smithton," he said.

I ran to the bunker to assist the doc with an operation. He stooped, under the dripping concrete ceiling, to assess a soldier's shattered leg by the oil lamplight. "Amputate," he said.

I applied the tourniquet and passed him the guillotine, a device designed for primitive amputations any medic could perform. The useless leg part fell to the floor and would be added to the next shared grave.

The patient only whimpered before he blacked out. When he recovered consciousness, he said his name was Charles, and others called him Charlie. He communicated with me later in unbelievable ways.

I considered options for dog cuisine. There'd been no recipes for dog broth during my lessons in sick room cooking at Malden Hospital. I briefly wavered between pit roasting and boiling and decided boiling would stretch the meat the furthest.

Into the pot it went, bones included. Our butcher cracked them with his trenching tool. Someone came up with a little salt, and a few scraggly weeds served as seasoning. The men had to imagine vegetables.

I was back and forth between surgery and cookery for a few hours, but it was worth it to see the boys eat. I fed broth to the weakest patients and gave meat to the rest.

"This is the best ever," one lad said.

I couldn't help thinking of Daddy's dog, Jack. I had no appetite that night.

"What does the meat taste like?" I asked.

"It reminds me of beef or mutton, more like beef, a little gamey, but not as strong as old mutton," one satisfied soldier told me.

"Not much fat came out in the broth."

"Naw, probably the animal was as hungry as us," he said.

"How does it compare to rat?"

"Different. Now with them, it depends what they're eating. If they're into garbage or sewers they're gamey, but if they're robbin' grain, they're delicate tastin'."

"I'm glad you liked it."

"The stew had a rich dark colour. Don't know how you do it, Sister. You've nothin' to work with." He lowered his voice. "It's rough having no rations," he said.

How right he was. We subsisted, in the middle of muddy fields, mostly on a beef and potato stew called slumgullian, when the supply trucks made it through. The canned corn willy and bully beef only lasted so long.

"But miss," another soldier said, "it's worse for morale when mail's delayed."

"Of course," I agreed.

I tensed from my stomach to my eyes to prevent crying, and next my brain mixed images: butcher and doctor, skinned dog and haemorrhaging leg, pocket knife and guillotine. It went on, a collage of recollections, visualizations, hallucinations.

I asked a soldier whether he ever mixed memories. "All the time, Sister. Mostly it's nightmares. Never know what's coming back."

**Marie Mossman**

# 24: Retreat

"Retreat."

The command came by carrier pigeon to take what we could carry from our CCS and immediately head for any safe haven. Our doctor decided we should each run without informing the others of our intended destination.

"I'll look out for you, Sister," Charles said as he was evacuated, the last person we transported out after the order.

An inner voice directed me to scramble to a farmhouse I'd seen, an island in the damp battleground between Ste. Lucy and our previous line.

*Too obvious. Won't everyone head there?*

The voice insisted, so I grabbed my field book, compass, and emergency kit and began my tramp. In the overcast night, a soft light led me, and my confidence built. My body tired, and yet found energy to slog on.

Unfortunately, I abandoned caution and promptly fell into a bomb crater. My heart pounded, and I gasped for air, but then a calm surrounded me and the voice said. "You have hands. Claw your way out."

I gouged footholds in the mud wall. Some grooves collapsed, but every third one provided purchase and eventually I lay splayed above the crater's edge.

"Get up, Sister." And I did.

The scene of unthinkable horrors continued, muddier than a Nova Scotian logging road in May. At first, the rats disgusted me. Later, I lacked energy for disgust as I made my way through the field strewn with rotting bodies and unattached limbs. I just plodded on.

Once I stepped on a corpse and putrid gas enveloped me. I readied myself, should it happen again, to use the technique taught me by an instructress in nursing school. "Block the connection between your nasal passages and your mouth. You won't throw up. It works every time."

I secured each step to avoid falling into another crater or a trench, or stepping on human parts. I worried whether I had judged the direction correctly, and wondered if the mysterious voice had abandoned me. I asked myself whether there was an end to the battlefields.

Near daybreak, I saw the shape of the farmhouse, a two and a half storied building, a common design on once prosperous farms. I prayed someone friendly lived there, then climbed three shaky wooden steps and rapped on the back entrance.

After a couple of minutes, the heavy door creaked open three inches. A large-boned man about my height stood there, and behind him a shorter matron. They both wore homespun nightshirts and bonnets. They were thin, like the hungry dog the men had eaten at the CCS.

I blurted out the phrase I'd been practising, "*Aidez-moi, s'il vous plaît.*" Would they take me in?

The door squeaked further open. They gestured me to enter. "*Madame l'infirmière...*" They recognized my nurse's uniform. With further gestures and little language, I understood they would hide me for one day.

The house used to have two staircases leading to the second story, a formal staircase and one for servants. The servant's staircase was hidden behind false walls on both floors. The whole downstairs hallway was covered in agèd looking paper and wood trim, so the false panel did not attract the eye.

Monsieur removed the panel, and revealed grey wooden stairs that curved upward. He told me to rest in the stairwell during daytime, and he would show me a safe route to the Allies once it was dark.

Madame offered to wash my clothes and clean my boots. I gratefully accepted the shelter, but would not part with my uniform as a Red Cross uniform was my best protection, especially the badge. But I did entrust my boots to her. Madame handed me a piece of dry bread and a bottle of water. A covered chamber pot sat on a stair.

"Close hooks here," Monsieur said, as he pointed out two hooks on the inside of the wall, that would hold the panel in place should any suspicious person arrive and decide to test its permanence.

I climbed into the space to rest as best I could on a set of wooden stairs. Would the Germans investigate this isolated farm?

At darkness, Monsieur hustled me from my closet, through the cellar, and out its low door. He urged me to wiggle feet-first into to a shallow disguised space under the floor of his wagon.

We moved away from the house, and stopped within minutes beside a stand of trees, where I heard him load a few sticks of wood onto the wagon: his explanation for being out, should he be stopped.

Then he told me to get out, handed me a hunk of bread, and pointed. "Quickly. The way to the Allies."

"Thank you, *Monsieur.*"

"Quick, quick. God help you."

# 25: In peace

Mid-August, 1918, I was stationed at a hospital south of Amiens, moved further west, and then moved again to #12 General at Rouen. Our moods wavered between despair from the mutilation of men in battle, and hope gleaned from reports the Germans were retreating. Spanish influenza attacked every nation in Europe and most of those beyond.

A letter came from "In France" and was dated August, 1918.

*My Dear Della,*
*Our letters always seem to cross, so I especially hope you receive this one in time to reply.*

*I expect leave soon, and it's my fervent wish to pass a quiet day with you (You remember our afternoon at Stonehenge?). Anywhere would be wonderful, but if we could meet away from the prying eyes and long noses of your colleagues, it would be heaven. Could you request a couple days off? You, too, would benefit from a short break. I know the hellish hours you angels work. If it would do any good, I'd go AWOL and plead your case in front of Matron.*

*There'll be an important person visiting you soon, and his assistant is a relative of mine from home who knows you by name and description. Amazing, isn't it? This cousin has promised to deliver you information on the date and place where we can find privacy for a day or two. So, Dear One, should any person of importance appear at your establishment, be sure to find yourself close to that person's aide.*
*Sincerely,*
*Charlie*

*France*
*August, 1918*
*My Dear Charlie,*
*How wonderful to receive a letter as it means you are alive, but I fear what you propose is reckless. We do not, however, live in normal conditions, and as you suggest, we work extraordinary hours. Just a glimpse of you would be an injection of honeyed adrenaline; however, do you not recall what happened after Stonehenge?*

*I agree to hear your cousin's message and to keep an open mind.*
*Sincerely,*

*Della*

I was granted leave and managed a ride to the village St. Petit Vic, south-west of my hospital. I was dropped off in mist at the Y where a street separated from the main road. The driver sped off in his Model T to make his deadline. I only just avoided the storm of mud and gravel his tires catapulted into the air.

In front of me a dirt road curved through an abandoned battleground toward a distant hill. I questioned whether I was being foolish, when I wasn't even sure if Charlie would be able to meet me. Soldiers had leave cancelled all the time.

I hiked around potholes in a stretch of mud, until I was close enough to discern, on the hillside, a stone building. The hotel was the size of a sea captain's home in Nova Scotia: two and a half stories. Behind the hotel rose a cluster of poplar trees. In front lay a cobblestone patio with two chairs and a bistro table. Yellow and orange wildflowers called toad-flax, and a red poppy, welcomed from their vase on the table.

The overture to "The Marriage of Figaro" exploded in my head when I saw Charlie hasten toward me. Where had he been?

We entered the *Hôtel des Peupliers* through a substantial front doorway. The air smelled divinely of coffee and baking. I saw a polished reception desk on our left and, on our right, a dining room where hung white lace curtains and hand crafted deer-horn candle holders. Wine glasses waited on six tables covered with red and white checked cloths, and on the tables, more candles ready to light.

Against the inner wall stood a piano, and in the middle of the wall facing it, a large stone hearth prepared with kindling and logs to light on a chilly evening. The building's interior was a rich dark wood with ceilings of cream plaster. In contrast to the building's unpainted, weathered exterior window frames, the interior was well-scrubbed, painted, and polished.

Charlie had requested separate rooms, but there was a problem.

The owner-operator said, "You've been allotted one room with two beds. I regret, that is all we can spare, given the current demand. Be assured, all persons here are discreet. Is it your pleasure to take the room?"

We looked questioning at each other and both of us shrugged and nodded.

"We'll take the room under my name only," Charlie said, then showed his ID and took the key.

"For a minimal charge, Madame will ensure the water and bathroom are heated, and impeccable. This service includes a towel and our special scented soap. Shall I place an order for one or two baths?"

"Yes, please," I replied.

Charlie held up two fingers. If ever I've smiled from ear to ear, it was then.

The owner nodded. "Two. My wife scents the soap herself with wild spring flowers."

We headed for the steep and narrow stairs.

A bath, what heaven! Any bath would be a luxury to me after months of chilly washes out of basins, in rooms lacking privacy.

I followed Madame down a narrow hallway to the bathroom. She opened the door to a heated private room. She provided a mini bar of the promised soap, a bathrobe, and a towel, soft, and pure white.

I had no desire to investigate how this tiny hotel continued to exist and could provide superior peacetime comforts.

"When you've finished, ring, and we will collect your clothes for washing. We do this for guests who support us in the war."

"Thank you so much. This bathroom is a dream."

"No, no, the pleasure is mine," she insisted. "I must go now. The guest in room three asked a hot broth be brought to her."

Charlie and I took the evening meal downstairs. I wore my plain wool dress.

"Your dress looks lovely on you," Charlie said.

But I knew it was plain, like me.

The owner served the meal. He and Madame must have worked sixteen hours a day, but nothing was trouble for them.

We ordered three courses: a soup of pureed potatoes, a thin slice of fried meat that may have been beef, and green lettuce leaves in a vinaigrette dressing.

An earthenware jug of red wine sat on our table. "The wine is local," Monsieur said.

Each course arrived with a basket of crusty whitish bread. In the peasant way, we tore off pieces and used them to wipe up every bit of juice on the plate.

The owner suggested a walk among the gardens and trees behind the hotel. "I assure you, Monsieur et Madame, it's perfectly safe."

Charlie and I strolled in peace among herbal beds, berry bushes, and apple trees as the sun went down. Along a pathway, we discovered a rustic bench where we enjoyed unusual quiet and the sight of a few trembling poplar leaves. Were they greeting us?

Again, I wondered how this island of serenity could exist, like intermission within the war theatre. It soothed the soul to be reassured the entire world was not mad.

The owner addressed us as we climbed the stairs to our room. "It's best to come down for breakfast by eight o'clock, because at that time the government permits us to serve butter and milk. Unfortunately, these foods are unavailable after nine o'clock." He shrugged. "Such is our life at this time. Good-night, my friends."

Our separate beds quickly became too chilly and lonely. As toasty as the bathroom had been, the bedroom was cold at night.

Charlie came to lie beside me, on top of the covers, and then under the covers. Our bodies close together, the desire within needed no kindling to ignite. We pressed more and more upon one another.

Finally, he murmured, "We must part."

"No, no. It'll be too cold."

But we did separate, and finally fell asleep. Our spirits strained to resist one another. During the night, Charlie merely brushed my shoulder and I clasped to him.

Eros had his way with us. My body exploded in new sensations. Eros laughed.

"What have I done?" I whimpered.

"You're my wife now, Del," Charlie said softly. "We'll make it official the next time we get leave."

"But, what if...?"

"Don't worry. I'll care for you."

"Charlie...there's something I've never told anyone."

"You don't have to tell me."

"Remember, I said I went to Boston to help my cousin, for the adventure."

"Mmm."

"That's true, but there was something else."

"Yes?"

"I wanted to get away from home. When I was in my teens, this neighbour man, the Deacon, was always bothering me, especially one time when he followed me into the barn. I got away from him, but afterwards I was always scared of him. He'd leer at me when others couldn't see, or he'd threaten, 'I'll have you one day.' I was always trying not to be alone, because of him."

"Why didn't you tell your parents?"

"They'd have said I was imagining things, or I must have done something to tempt him. Everyone thought he was a righteous man."

"You're safe from him now."

"He made it difficult for me to trust men."

"And now I've taken advantage of you. I'm sorry, Della."

"No, Charlie. Don't feel that way. I gave myself to you. It's different."

"You're precious to me, Del. We'll marry and I'll care for you."

We fell asleep, our bodies close together the rest of the night.

Early morning noises. Could have been anything. Prisoner escapees? Deliveries?

We went down to breakfast on time. I wasn't going to miss the chance for fresh croissants with butter, Madame's plum jam, and coffee with hot milk. Fifty years later, my mouth salivates at the thought of it.

The owner served us. "Madame is a bit unwell." Madame was not seen that day nor the next. I could hear coughing from the hosts' quarters.

"Sister, I beg of you, what should I do for my wife? She has a fever, is dizzy, and has such muscle aches and joint pains."

"Try to reduce her fever by sponging her with tepid water. If you have an aspirin, give her one for pain, and try to have her drink water, herbal teas, or broth."

"There must be more I can do."

"The doctors in the hospitals can do no more for her. They sometimes take fluid samples, but that's for their research. Rest yourself, whenever you can."

I softened my voice and slightly shook my head. "Matron won't be pleased if I return having caught influenza, or if I'm late. I can't stay to nurse her."

~

Charlie and I took one last walk in the back garden. Once more we marvelled at the unusually clear weather and quiet in this area, and then it was time to return to duties.

We walked hand in hand to the main road.

"Della, take care of yourself." He pulled a gun from his pocket.

"Charlie!" I lurched away from him.

"I want you to have this. It's a Browning, American made, reliable."

"No, Charlie, I couldn't ever use it."

"Please. I'll know you're safer."

I shook my head. His dear eyes filled with tears.

He repeated we were married, kissed my cheek and turned toward the hotel.

I was still reeling from the extraordinary weekend when my ride arrived, as scheduled.

There was another passenger in the car. He certainly wasn't a common solider. Just as well, considering what happened during the return to my hospital.

# 26: Going in

An older gentleman in fatigues occupied the front passenger seat and exuded the confidence that comes with authority. An officer, or member of the brass?

"No time to spare," the driver, a teenager, said. "Our passenger's in a hurry. Don't ask."

He helped me through a canvas-covered entryway into the wooden box that formed a back compartment. There was a square porthole on each side-wall, and the holes were covered from the outside by a sliding wood shutter. I anticipated fresh air and a rewind of familiar scenery.

A wooden crate was nailed to one side-wall below the porthole. "You'll have to sit on the crate, Sister, and hold on tight or you'll be thrown around something terrible."

"I have to report for duty by nineteen hundred hours. Let's carry on," I said and braced my mind and body for a long, hellish ride.

Why was such a distinguished looking man riding in a common vehicle? I concluded he wished to avoid the attention of spies in farmhouses along the way.

The motor in the front whined until I wondered if the men were deaf, but I knew better than to say anything. From turns the vehicle made, I guessed we were taking a different route than we'd travelled to the *Hôtel des Peupliers* so I attempted to slide open the shutters. They moved only the tiniest crack.

I clenched my teeth, and then relaxed them when I breathed in the saltiness of sea air. Glimpses of sand reminded me of rumours about the coastal dunes being penetrated like an anthill by tunnels hiding artillery and troop shelters. Other times, slivers of trees flashed by, then remnants of farms, and, saddest of all, familiar man-made wastelands.

We sped until 'flap, flap, flap' replaced the whining. Must have been hitting forty-five miles per hour between potholes.

"Shit!" our driver exclaimed.

I remained as silent as any sane woman could.

I heard the driver march around to the toolbox fixed to the passenger running board, and then rummage in the box. No need to repeat the officer's increasingly foul language. I wasn't learning much.

"What we need, Sir, is a fan belt, and there's no spare in the kit. If there were any trees here, I could jury-rig one from the inner bark, but the last trees were miles back."

"Fuck you," said the officer. "If that's the best you can do, run back until you find a tree with bark, a horse and wagon, or a truck to commandeer. Hear me?"

"Excuse me, gentlemen," I said.

There was a startled silence. I pressed on.

"I've heard, in an emergency, one might fashion a belt out of a stocking. May I offer mine?"

"Quite right, Sister. You may save the day," the officer said.

I handed my stocking through the canvas door to our driver. He looked down as he took it.

A peek around, and I saw a house I didn't recognize from my ride out to the hotel. "Shall I give you the other one, just in case?"

"Not necessary."

I removed my other stocking, crammed it into my pocket, and then fished my wool dress out of my bag and wrapped it around my legs for warmth.

Our driver tied on the improvised belt, and we sped off a smidgen more carefully than we had previously travelled—until a tiny whine under the bonnet increased to a full blast complaint, and then expired as the improvised fan belt split. The truck rolled to a halt.

The brass let off a stream of expletives that would have intimidated Kaiser William himself. Pity the king wasn't within hearing range.

*If they knew how hard it is to get new stockings!*

"This may help." I held the remaining stocking out to the driver. His face turned red as he took it.

"Do keep the good parts of the worn one. Never know, we may have to splice some bits together later on."

"Yes, Sister."

Would we get to the hospital on time for my duty? I foresaw no dinner and shuddered at the thought of Matron's temper.

Our driver tied the hose in place and in minutes we again headed northwest. A prickly aura from the passenger up front kept me alert. I breathed deeply of the homey sea air.

I mused whether Cousin Geoffrey had ever been in the region, living like a rabbit under the dunes. And why were we zigzagging our way back? It was taking longer than the ride to the hotel.

We travelled a less reckless pace than earlier, so I relaxed my body somewhat on the wooden crate.

Two thirds the way to my hospital, a new blast of curses accosted my ears. Our driver stopped the vehicle. "May as well get out, Sister."

Steam escaped from the engine. "I topped the oil this morning, so it's not likely that. Could be the fancy new fan belt is slipping."

"Can you tighten it?"

"Have to. Pray it lasts, Sister. Hunt around for water, will you? I'll take the cap off as soon as this baby cools down some." He pointed to the radiator.

"Things happen in threes. Maybe we'll be okay from here on," I said.

We had stopped in a small stand of pine trees. I scouted up the road for water and took the opportunity to dash behind a tree. The officer headed to the other side of the road, and I smiled to myself. We had one need in common.

A familiar sound. A French ambulance appeared through the mist, from the north. Our hood was propped up and our driver gesticulated to indicate our problem. Our allies pulled out a couple of wine bottles filled with water.

"The only time I've been happy to see water in a wine bottle," said the officer.

I exchanged a few niceties in French with our unexpected rescue team. My efforts were well accepted, so my chest expanded as all hands waved good-bye.

The last leg of my journey I worried about Matron's reception. No one knew the true nature of my leave, but would Matron send a negative report to Stimson? I already had a black mark against me from Fargo.

Our hospital, a collection of low sheds, sat on a tragic mix of mud, blood, and despair. Within the buildings our soldiers suffered, pawns of their leaders. I had pledged to care for these remnants of men and was returning late for duty. I fretted like the knot in our improvised fan belt repeated its circuit.

The driver helped me out of the back of our vehicle and handed me my bag.

Then the officer appeared beside us. "Soldier, I'm going in with Sister."

"Sir, I must report to Matron," I said.

"Yes, and I'll speak to her, too."

I approached Matron's desk. She looked up, a grim expression on her tired face. "Sister,—"

Then she stood. "Colonel, I—"

He interrupted her. "Matron, good evening. This sister rescued us today. She's a heroine, and is not to be punished in any way if she has overstayed her time."

"Yes, sir."

"Your report to Chief Nurse Stimson will state only that Sister returned after providing exceptional service to our cause."

"Certainly, sir."

"Ensure she receives dinner before she resumes duty this evening. Understand?"

"Yes, sir!"

He turned and strode toward the door. Matron did not look pleased. Her mouth was still open, and her eyebrows raised.

# 27: Such fatigue

Matron's face returned to its weary and furrowed presentation immediately the colonel was out of sight. "Very well, Sister Della, you may take a plate from the kitchen, and serve yourself a hot tea." She lowered her chin and focused her eyes on my bare legs. "Then put on stockings and return to duty."

"Yes, Matron. Thank you."

"You're late for dinner, Sister," said the server.

"I know, but Matron ordered me to request a meal before night duty."

"Lucky I have one ration left, only because some poor bastard couldn't eat."

She plopped a mess of gristly stew on my plate. I stretched my senses to smell beef. By comparison to meals at the *Hôtel des Peupliers*, army slop was suitable for pigs, but I'd eaten little during the day. I swallowed every blob of gravy.

Night duty proceeded as normal for this month when our men were sacrificing themselves to regain territory from the Bosch. My body, however, felt unusually tired. Was I too old for wartime nursing? I forced myself to perform regular jobs, to plump pillows, administer painkillers, straighten blankets, read to patients.

"Thank you, Sister." "When you have time, Sister, might you....?" How uncomplaining they were, men wounded in a war organized by others.

This tiredness was different, right to my bone marrow, so I summoned mental strength for work until the shift's end.

Then an orderly appeared. "Matron says you're to stay on. Your relief nurse hasn't come back."

I leaned on a post for support and forced myself to begin day duties. I changed dressings and administered drugs, but at half my normal pace. I had no energy to feel joy when the relief nurse did show up.

"So sorry, Sister, the vehicle broke down on my return." Who was I to question that?

My hand patted a teabag in my breast pocket, Lipton's, sent from friends in Boston. I'd already used the bag twice, so didn't fear it might keep me awake.

I stopped at surgery for hot water from the boiler and continued to my cubicle. A partial hand wash, then I slumped onto my bed, tea in hand.

I'd never experienced such fatigue. What was its cause? I lay on the bed with my clothes on as usual and fell asleep immediately.

Half a cup of cold tea on my table greeted my waking eyes the next afternoon. I couldn't waste tea, so I drank it.

Next, I reached for my basin and vomited until my stomach turned inside out. Only bile escaped with the last lurch.

"Della, are you all right?" said a voice from a nearby cubicle.

"Must have eaten something bad. I'll be okay."

I remembered my nights with Charlie at *des Peupliers*, and worried I might have morning sickness. I worried the brass would send me home, dishonourable discharge. What if Charlie wouldn't marry me?

I had always felt superior to loose women. I was no better. I thought of 'doing something'.

*No, couldn't live with abortion on my conscience. I'll go somewhere different in the States. Pretend I'm widowed.*

"Time to report for night duty," a sing-song voice reminded me from outside my cubicle.

I forced myself up, splashed cold water on my face and hands and walked the short distance outdoors to our ward. There, dozens of patients were placed two to a bed because of our current intake.

"You don't look well, Sister Della."

"I'll be okay when I get going."

But I wasn't.

# 28: London

Dizziness hit. I remember only snippets of speech and scenes from then until days later.

"She dropped!"

"Get Matron."

"Has a fever."

"That dreadful...."

"Strong. Might survive."

"...next train to London...."

I was jostled while shadows bustled around me. Mechanical noises, whispering and shouting. At one time, I was aware of water lapping against something. I didn't care. I whimpered like a dying horse.

Later, I became alert in an airy ward with thirty-five other cots. The room had a high ceiling, proper plaster walls painted a light green, and large windows.

Four nurses distributed clean linen, meals, soothing potions. They spoke with an American accent and discretely managed sponge baths and administered drugs. Patients looked pale and thin, but they had all their limbs.

"Where am I?'

"London. Notes say you collapsed at work. Your signs were consistent with Spanish flu, so your matron had you transported here. You're over the worst."

"I must get back."

"Just as well you want to return, 'cause your matron requested we re-habilitate you as soon as possible. She thinks highly of your skills. Your job now, Sister, is to regain strength."

She was right about me being weak, this young lady in her grey linen dress and white apron.

"It must be interesting being a patient when you're a nurse and know how things should be done. Have you ever been a patient before, Sister Della?"

"When I was in training."

"What was it like?"

"I hated it when a nurse whipped the curtains open to wake me in the morning."

"Anything else?"

"They wanted me to go to sleep when I felt like reading. They'd come in, close the curtains and turn the lights off. Routine ruled."

"What did the staff do right?"

"My doctor and nurses worked skilfully to rid me of my appendix."

Her voice softened to a compassionate tone. "You'd like staff to care as well about your preferences, and your emotions?"

"Yes. I know that's not always possible."

"Where were you?"

"Malden, near Boston."

"Malden Hospital has an excellent reputation. Sister Della, we'll get you up and moving soon, maybe tomorrow."

"I feel better now."

"We don't want a relapse. You've just become alert."

I had been sitting, propped by pillows, and at the mention of relapse, I lay back.

Sister went about her duties and I berated myself for my moral lapse with Charlie, my body's failure, and uselessness to the war effort. Sleep overtook me, but my mind remained active. I heard airplanes attack. I discovered I was pregnant.

Daylight exposed my worries for the nightmares they had been.

I was tidying the dishes on my tray the day two nurses appeared beside my bed with an empty wheelchair. "Sister Della, we're moving you to a ward for more active patients."

They helped me into the chair. "Let's roll."

Patients in the ward called out, "Good for you, Sister Della!"

"See you over there soon."

"You're grinning," one of the nurses said.

They stopped the wheelchair short of my new bed and helped me stand up. I took two steps, with a sister at either elbow.

"See, you're walking now. Tomorrow, we'll get you walking more and maybe working. What do you think?"

"I'd like it." I settled between ironed sheets.

From my bed, I had a good look around the new ward the next morning. A nurse walked in with an armload of clean linen. She introduced herself as Sister Marian.

"Is this a new hospital?" I asked.

"No, but our army updated everything and took it over from the British the first of this month. It's now a base hospital."

"You all wear similar pins."

"Yes, we're Colorado State University grads. The orderlies and rest of support staff come from Denver. We've lots of fun together on days off."

"It's calm here, not crowded, compared to where I've worked on the Continent."

"We keep busy enough. Would you feel up to helping me put away this linen?"

"Of course. I'd like something useful to do."

"We're short two nurses today. The dreadful influenza. Be sure to tell me if you're tired."

"I will."

"When you feel up to it, you can go over to St. Ann's Church hall, nearby. The rector lets us use it as a recreation hut."

"What's there?"

"A library and a writing room with paper and pens. And a billiard room. Pool. Do you play?"

"Never have. But I love to read, and should write home."

I also wanted to write to Charlie. He wouldn't know I was in London. Any letter from him would be slow getting to me.

"The hospital has thirty-three acres," continued Sister Marian.

"That's huge for a city hospital."

"Yes. A lot of the land's covered by other ward blocks, but there's room for walking outdoors in relative quiet. You should see the quaint stone wall. We'll get you out there when you're stronger."

"Can't be too soon for me. I'm not used to lazing around."

"Others are waking now, so I must see to them. You should rest a bit, Sister, even if you don't want to. You've been up a while already this first morning."

"You're right." I sighed.

"Thank you for helping with the linen. I've enjoyed getting to know you."

"We might have a lot in common."

"Maybe we're kindred spirits, Sister Della."

"Possibly." I'd not heard of a kindred spirit outside of books, but thought it a charming concept. Perhaps I needed a kindred spirit. I wanted to emulate this nurse, knew I'd prefer to be more soft, like her.

I slept until she wakened me for lunch. I sipped broth, nibbled at a Spam sandwich, and drank tea with milk. I planned on saving part of my sandwich for dinnertime.

"No need to save that bit, Sister Della. We'll send it to the pigs. Adequate supplies come from the States," Sister Marian said.

I toddled to the recreation hut the next day. In the first room, young men chalked their cues with the seriousness of battle strategists.

"Could you please direct me to the writing room?" I asked.

One lad removed the cigarette from his mouth. "Yes, Sister, down the hallway and hang left."

The writing room was dignified, with two large writing desks of fine dark wood and shelving with paper, envelopes, and a notice: "A generous person has donated stamps for the use of patients. Apply to the Administration block for any stamps you need."

I wondered whether 'Apply to' meant there would be a form to fill out.

I sat on the high-backed wooden chair placed by one of the desks, opened a bottle of ink, and took up a pen. Outside the window, a shaft of sunlight shone on a quivering plane tree leaf. I decided it was waving to me.

> *England*
> *August, 1918*
> *My Dearest Charlie,*
>
> *Currently, I' m recovering in a hospital away from the battle area. I've had influenza and assure you my strength improves daily. It's quiet and safe here and the care is exceptional.*
>
> *I hope you're safe and well. Worry about you, however, is never far from my thoughts. It calms me to picture you, the honest, engaging person that you were on our first outing, and the gentle man you revealed when we last met. We have such wonderful memories and plans together. How I long for news of you!*
>
> *If you write c/o where I was, your letter might be forwarded.*
>
> *Ever praying for your safety,*
> *Sincerely,*
> *Della*

I wrote a brief, reassuring note to Katherine, then went to post my letters at the Administration Block.

"Why do we have to 'apply' for stamps? What happens if we are turned down?"

The clerk looked blank for a moment. "Oh, I see. You're American. In proper English, 'apply' clearly means 'ask for'. You ask and we provide. The donor wants us to ensure they're actually used by patients for their own letters."

I displayed my letter as evidence, received my stamp with thanks, and posted the letter.

As I turned to leave, the clerk added, "Don't overdo it, Sister. We need you to get well."

I decided to check out the library another day.

# 29: Play tomorrow

I returned to the recreation hut after a few more restful days. Again, men and women were playing billiards and they asked me to join in.

"Thanks for inviting me. I'll play another time."

"Okay, Sister."

The library invited with a soft couch, a desk, and two easy chairs facing each other. Yesterday's newspaper lay on a table, and shelves of books covered two walls.

I opened a few novels. Their bookplates read "Donated by the kindness of Lord Beaton", or "From the library of Lady Stoppa", or "Provided by monies collected by students of the London Open Air School".

A green volume, published in 1908, caught my eye. I took it in hand and sat down, remembering how I'd first encountered the term "kindred spirit" in this very version of *Anne of Green Gables*. What would people at the hospital think if I told them the author's husband was a distant relative? They'd think I was bragging.

I supposed half the people in the Maritimes claimed a connection to L.M. Montgomery, but my relationship to her still made me proud, as though I had helped her on her way. Funny, that. She probably had never heard of me. How many people felt a connection to someone who had achieved fame?

I thought it wonderful, how Montgomery turned her lonely childhood into stories that gave pleasure to thousands and how she continued to write after she married. I too wanted to serve as an inspiration to other women. Show them they could have a career.

I had avoided love and marriage until I met Charlie, but Montgomery married, kept her imagination free, and continued to write.

"Hello, Sister." A young woman with an armload of books to shelve had paused near me.

"Oh, good morning."

"Is the book interesting?"

"Yes, it's popular. It tells about an orphan girl and how she...well, I won't give away the story, but it charms most people who read it, and it describes Prince Edward Island in Canada, not far from where I grew up."

"I've heard of it, but never had time to read until now. Are you planning to take the Anne book out?"

"No, I've read it a couple times. Here, feel free."

She left with the book and a smile.

Life had been good back in Nova Scotia when I was young. I visualized East Cove where the road between Halifax and Lunenburg ran close to the Atlantic Ocean, and thought about how the moods of the sea influenced our daily lives. Our salt box house sat on its drumlin overlooking the road, and across it, the sea. Tides fed us energy. We didn't get energy from the tides, but I imagined it. Actually, we did, I decided.

Mother was always working in the house or gardens. Father and my brothers laboured on our mixed farm, and they fished. I longed for our vegetable gardens, currant and gooseberry bushes, our apple trees, the wild berry bushes, especially my favourite, huckleberry.

My heart leapt at the image of Blackie in our barn of rough-hewn timbers.

I pictured Father standing in his dory in his homemade oilskins while he rowed to our sailboat to fish. I saw him in his winter woollens, heading out to cut wood with my brothers. They took the sled to our woodlot back in the forest.

Our days were long and fully occupied with work, except Sundays when we donned our best outfits to go to church. We sat in the second and third pews from the front, all twelve of us. Those pews belonged to us.

Mother truly believed cleanliness was next to godliness. She made sure we were scrubbed, ironed, and tidily coiffed. She kept our home orderly, with a place for everything and everything in its place. Mother's training eased my acceptance of the strict cleanliness demanded in nursing.

We ate well at home: in winter, our own root vegetables, sauerkraut, pickled beans and pickled turnip; in spring, we gathered dandelion greens. How I liked them with lots of butter and vinegar. In summer we had tender vegetables like lettuce, cucumbers and tomatoes. We butchered our own meat and turned it into sausages, bacon or corned meat for the winter. We dried, salted or smoked fish. The men hunted moose and trapped rabbits. Best of all, we were healthy and lived peacefully.

Then an image of the Deacon flitted by.

*His soul is dry rot. If I ever see him again, I won't be afraid.*

And I knew I wouldn't be, at least not like in my youth. I felt as safe in the London hospital as I would ever be.

A lad brought in a copy of *The Times* for that mid-August day. "Enemy's Flanders Retreat" and "German Defeat On Aisne-Oise Front".

I thought of the cost of our advances. My mind flashed back to the horror of our field hospitals, the hammering of guns, the smells of rotting flesh, feces, urine, blood; bodies with missing limbs, eyeballs hanging out of their sockets, men crying for their mothers, begging to die, pleading for one kiss before they died.

*Stop it, Del. Be where you are, here, among civilized people, warm, fed, safe.*

I signed out *Delia Blanchflower*, by a new author, Mrs Humphry Ward. It promised to be witty and romantic. Just what I needed.

"Tomorrow, I'll play tomorrow," I said as I walked past the happy group playing billiards.

But I didn't play billiards tomorrow.

# 30: Spanish influenza

My heart reached out to Charlie with startling force as I walked the short distance across the grounds toward my ward. Was he thinking of me?

My body felt chilled. I commented to a passing nurse who carried a grey sweater over her arm, "That woolly looks cosy."

"Yes. I don't need it this morning, but I'll be glad to have it when the days turn cooler. The grey goes perfectly with our uniform. All us Denver nurses were issued sweaters by the Red Cross, because of the open corridors."

My chill disappeared before I reached my bed, but suddenly a burning fever overtook me.

The ward nurse said. "Sister Della, your face is red. Are you feeling okay?"

"Not quite, Sister."

She consulted briefly in a low voice with a colleague. I overheard: 'gauze mask' and 'new contagious cubicles'.

They transferred me to a cubicle. It was formed by sheets hung around my bed to make a tiny room in a ward filled with similar cubicles.

A nurse explained. "We've been directed to take the same precautions with the Spanish influenza as we use with tuberculosis. You must have complete rest until the fever passes. Now, don't you worry about a thing."

My mind, however, wouldn't still. I saw Charlie, blood spurting from a head wound, pleading. "Del, help me." I saw Charlie and me. We walked, hand in hand. I laughed at one of his jokes. We stopped and he whispered into my ear. "I love you."

~

"You've been here four days, Sister, and your fever's down. If it stays down overnight, that'll be forty-eight hours and we'll move you out of this cubicle in the morning. You've had a relapse, mostly the fever this time. You must rest, though. No gadding about until your strength returns."

"Was it too much, that I walked to the recreation hut?"

"Not at all, if you felt up to it. The infection comes back on its own schedule. The unlucky ones, younger people usually, don't make it through the first attack. Your age is an advantage. Now, you rest."

I was returned to my initial ward.

"Hello, Sister Della. What've you been doing they've brought you back here?" asked one of the few patients I recognized.

"Missed your charm," I replied.

A chuckle rippled around the ward.

I noticed the staff were using stronger-smelling antiseptic solutions than before and I counted only three nurses on duty for the forty patients.

A nurse came by. "Sister Della, would you like the *Delia Blanchflower* book you signed out a few days ago?"

"Thank you, but I don't feel up to reading."

"It looks like a cracker book. Might keep your spirits up. Mind if I peek at it now and then? I'll keep it aside for you."

"Go ahead and read it. It'll be days before I can."

I longed for Charlie, or for a letter from him, then felt guilty, because I hadn't thought of him enough the last few days. When I was sick, I withdrew into my own body and didn't think of others, like the more selfish soldiers. I remembered how some of the wounded soldiers in France would say, "When you have time..." or "If you can manage to...." while other soldiers would appear unaware I was working at my limit and would demand immediate attention.

War news told only of Germany's defeats. If we were winning all the time, our mail should have gotten through, yet I received no letters from Charlie, no news of him. He wouldn't have gotten my letter yet, but if he were in a good situation, he would have sent a note to me, and the hospital would have forwarded it to me in London.

I reminded myself that mail frequently went astray, could take months to get to the right place, and the army gave priority to letters for the men in the trenches. What could I do to find out how Charlie was?

I also dredged up energy to worry about pregnancy. What woman wouldn't? I knew the wisest action was to keep quiet until my body produced a clear sign.

"Sister, your bed is desperately needed for a patient who is sicker than you," a nurse told me as she moved me back to the ward for stronger patients. "You must continue bed rest, though, until you feel more energy."

Sleeping and awake, I continued my loop of worries as though my mind had created a hellish torture chamber. It whipped me from one painful device to the next, around and around the circuit.

~

"Feel up to reading today?"

I reached for the offered *Blanchflower* book. "Thank you, yes, I'd like that."

But first I read the letter that had just arrived.

**Marie Mossman**

# 31: Spinsters talking

*East Cove,*
*June 25, 1918*
*Dear Della,*

*Hope you are keeping well. We all worry about you, and pray the war and flu epidemic will soon end. Maybe when your work in Europe is completed you'll return to East Cove and we'll finish the crazy quilt we started when we were sixteen. Once in a while I put aside a fabric scrap that might fit into the top. It's in my cedar chest and will remain there until you come back.*

*There's not much to tell from here, except a fascinating story I overheard. You remember how Aunt Ellen and Aunt Sarah are 'oh, so proper'? Years ago, they made a quintal of excuses so Rebecca couldn't join the Canadian Advanced Tatters' Society: "Her work isn't tidy enough." "She doesn't finish the edges like everyone else does." "She uses the wrong colours." and so on. The unspoken reason? Rebecca was Jewish.*

I put the letter down and wondered if those old biddies would think differently if they served a couple of weeks in a field hospital. Then I continued reading.

*You must remember, too, the old spinsters talking about their father (our grandfather) who always wore a small knitted cap, and his favourite wrap on his shoulders when he sat on his rocking chair. He spent a lot of time there, when elderly, mumbling to himself. Well, our dear aunts recently got it into their head to clean the attic in the old family home, and what did they find? Lots of junk, but also a small wooden box decorated with old German writing. In the box, was a tiny torah, and a booklet of Jewish prayers! I'll leave it to you to guess what Grandfather was mumbling. (I thought you should know, but all this is very 'hush- hush' and I'd like to keep it that way.)*
*P.S. I'm sending you some Lipton tea in those little bags. They're much 'in' here and handy, but I still think real leaves make better tea.*

*Must get back to the chores,*
*Yours sincerely,*
*Charlene*

Tears formed in my eyes. The secret about Grandfather paralleled my keeping quiet about my German name and background. What was wrong with being a Jew or a German, or a German Jew, for that matter? The good or evil you did was what counted.

If this letter found me, one from Charlie could. Why was there no news from him? Was he injured or sick? I tried not to think about what might have happened. Besides, I'd only been in London two weeks.

*Char has a beautiful hand, but she still makes an awkward capital G.*

I chuckled at my thought, and at myself, for being such an incurable school marm. While the Canadian Advanced Tatters' Society was known affectionately as CATS by its all-female membership, the menfolk also called it CATS, but with lips turned down at the corners, eyes rolled up-ward and a nod their chums understood.

I pictured our righteous aunts, their intolerance of children, and un-tidiness, and of any activity other than reading on Sundays. They kept their stringy hair in tight buns, wore sombre colours, and maintained ramrod posture.

I knew others saw me too much like my aunts. Had Charlie changed me, at least a little?

Rebecca, whose husband owned the shoe store in Easton, handed a sweet to any child who came in.

Mother would say to me. "Rebecca can turn her hand to any sort of fancy work, and her tatting is as fine as anything the ladies in CATS turn out." But I'm sure Mother never defended Rebecca to my aunts.

I never saw Rebecca at *any* ladies' group, and I wondered if my aunts' attitudes would change after the war.

*Now, what is this book from the library about?*

# 32: Stuffing out

The nurses expected good news.

"Sisters, I'm to inform you that nurses of the American Army have been warranted. The army has created the grade "nurse". This means you are below a cadet and above a sergeant-major. As such, you are placed in authority over all non-commissioned men. This information will be reported shortly in the September issue of *The British Journal of Nursing*."

Charlie will have to obey me!

I smiled at the thought, and immediately longed to hear from him.

"There's one more happy announcement. An outing to Colebrook Lodge is confirmed for tomorrow, and I've procured a bus for the day, so there'll be room for all who are well enough to go. Sister Marian will accompany you and take care of any medical concerns."

"Matron Best, could you tell us about Colebrook Lodge?" a patient, Sister Dorothy from New York, asked.

"Certainly, Sister. It's an American Red Cross Rest House for convalescent nurses, located on Putney Heath, across London. The gardens are extensive, so you may wish to spend much of your day outdoors, if the weather is suitable. Do take your new cardigans. This *is* England. I believe Matron at Colebrook has reserved the cricket field for us. Dress appropriately for exercise."

A buzz broke out.

"With my luck, it'll be a horse bus, or a blanket bus. No seats, no windows, just stacks of blankets," said Sister Edith, petite, a former secretary.

"Or a bunch of wooden benches on the back of a lorry," Sister Hélène said.

"What'll we wear?" Sister Nancy worried.

"Uniforms, I imagine. What else do we have?" Dorothy replied.

"Wonder if the food's any good there?"Sister Annette said.

The motor-omnibus had the letters LGOC across the front, and Sister Edith wondered what the letters meant.

"London General Omnibus Company, Sister," came the answer from the driver.

"It's painted red, so cheery," I said.

"And look at the fancy curved staircase. I'm going up for air," Dorothy said. A few women followed her up.

My colleagues on the lower level with me chatted on. Our bus was a beauty, an open-topped double-decker. We enjoyed the large windows all around and the heavily-padded seats. The chassis looked as tough as a Model T, though the bodywork was wooden.

Our driver, still in his white summer uniform, was protected from the weather by only a canopy over his head.

There was also a uniformed male conductor. "The company's started to hire women conductors, but of course, they get paid less," he said.

We tried not to dwell on how thin and dreary the Londoners walking on sidewalks looked, or their gauze masks; instead, we chatted or read publicity posters out loud and exclaimed about the products they advertised. Wright's Coal Tar Soap, Tatcho ("What on earth is that?"), or Maples bedding ("How do you make bedding out of maples?").

A half hour later we arrived at Colebrook Lodge.

"The seats upstairs were hard," Dorothy reported.

The lodge, a mansion refurbished to accommodate thirty nurses, welcomed us with a large arrangement of fresh flowers on either side of the entrance hallway. I liked, especially, the wide veranda that overlooked the cricket pitch and surrounding lawn.

On our arrival, Colebrook's matron hosted a morning tea before suggesting we might enjoy a game of garden cricket. She countered our stunned stares with, "I'll send Jennie from the dining room to set up your game. Out to the lawn with you, now."

Eight of us traipsed toward the level green grass, and the more timid nurses stood on the veranda. Jennie appeared in a flash, carrying a bat and tennis balls, talking on the fly to us players. "I expect you girls to be working on your nervous nineties before lunch, 'cause I gotta go in then."

None of us knew what she meant, and she blasted on talking to herself and to us, as she whipped us into positions to play cricket. I judged the wickets, already set on the lawn, were about fifteen yards apart.

She pointed to Edith and Annette. "You two are first batters for the first innings." Edith looked at the rest of us, and rolled her eyes.

Jennie pointed with the bat to the wicket where one batter would hit the ball toward trees. "Over to the far wicket, one of you. T'other one stands at the other end for now."

"You be silly." Jennie said, as she sent Hélène to stand by the batters' wicket. Hélène danced and waved her arms, playing the silly part, as she thought she was instructed. Nancy's giggling at Hélène's antics started the rest of us off.

Jennie picked me as first bowler, advising me, "I wouldn't try a googly this first innings."

Dorothy and Nancy became pair three, leg side fielders, and as in a three-legged race, they ran toward their station, laughing on the way.

Jennie told Ina, "You play offside fielder to start. Out you go."

Then Jennie turned to Sister Marian, who stood on the field, but closer to the veranda than the rest of us had been. "Sister, will you join the action, or do you prefer playing twelfth man?"

Sister Marian's brow furrowed for a second. "I'll join in. Never wanted to play a man."

Giggles burst out again.

"We need a second offside fielder," Jennie said. She pointed to the space opposite Ina on the lawn.

She told us, "We'll rotate positions every time both batters make a hit. Don't want any ducks in our game. I'm the ump. Got it?"

She turned to the sisters on the veranda. "You lot over there: we expect proper cheering from you, see?" Then, she said politely to me. "Throw the ball."

I hesitated an instant. *How? Underhand? Over?*

"Throw the bleeding ball," she bellowed. It landed halfway to the other wicket. Two more of my attempts failed, and silence enveloped the cheering squad on the veranda.

Jennie picked up the wicket from my end and replanted it about halfway closer to the other end. "Try now, Sister," she said in a kindly voice.

The ball flew to the opposite wicket, where petite Edith whacked it with the bat. Our audience cheered our hits, and laughed with us when we goofed.

Jennie rotated our positions, so every player managed to score at least one run, before Colebrook's matron walked out to the veranda and gave Jennie a nod.

Jennie announced, "As Umpire, I declare everyone a winner. I've received a message from Matron. She invites you into the dining room for lunch."

Once inside, where the tables were set with linen, silverware, and English china teapots, Jennie converted herself into an efficient waitress. The cook must have been English because we had clear soup and then meat pie, followed by sandwich cake and tea.

"I used to think cricket was stuffy, but it isn't, really," Sister Ina, from New York, said.

"We sure took the stuffing out of it! Remember when Sister Hélène tripped on her skirt and went bottoms up!" Nancy said, but she didn't mention the grass stains on Hélène's uniform.

"You all had a good laugh at me. I reckon I've done my good deed for the day," Hélène said.

Annette said, "You know what they say, 'laughter's the best'—"

"Medicine," twenty voices chimed in.

"Hey girls, let's go over how to play that silly cricket game," Dorothy said.

"It's like baseball, 'cept the pitcher's a bowler, and she throws the ball toward the batter, who's a striker. Not much more to know, the way we played it," Edith said.

"A little bit more. You should have eleven on your team, though we didn't," I said.

"And when your team's at bat, two take turns being the striker, but the one who's not batting stays way at the far end and is called the non-striker," Dorothy said.

"Enough already," from Ina. "It's not a game you can explain."

Shortly afterwards, Jennie relayed her matron's direction for us to head for our double-decker.

Matron emerged from Colebrook Lodge at the last minute, with a re-laxed smile. She said. "You've been wonderful sports. You've lifted my spirits today. Safe journey through these perilous weeks to come." As she waved us good-bye, her smile appeared forced.

On the bus, conversation turned to a common interest.

"Wasn't the food the best? Fresh milk with the tea and real butter on the bread," Annette said..

"I liked the real ham in the sandwiches this morning better than the meat pie," I said.

"What did you think of the dark stuff? Marmite, I think they called it," Dorothy said.

"Yuck," from Nancy and Annette.

"I liked it. My mom's English and we ate it at home," Edith said.

"Limey. You're half a limey."

Giggles.

"Darned right I am. That's why I signed up," Edith retorted.

"Sisters, you're getting serious, and that's not allowed on this bus," Sister Marian said.

"Hey, Della, cheer up. Didn't you have a good time today?" Nancy asked.

"Yes." But something heavy was happening inside me.

"Show it. Let's see a smile."

"Okay." Even I knew my tone was flat.

"Lunch was cracker, wasn't it?" Annette tried to cheer me.

"Yes," I said. I didn't know what had happened. A dark cloud had entered right into my brain and my heart.

*What can I do?*

"We'll let you be, then," Annette said.

"Del, you're still looking glum. What's wrong?" Sister Marian's voice conveyed concern, like a real friend would. We were halfway back to our hospital.

"Don't know." I wanted to crawl into bed and be by myself.

"Maybe dinner'll cheer you up. Matron Best said she'd have a special one waiting when we got back," Annette said.

"Shall we sing, girls? How about 'Pack up Your Troubles in Your Old Kit Bag'?" Dorothy said.

The others sang their way back across London. I heard their cheer, but my mind ran a loop of worries.

Where and how was Charlie? Was I in the family way? When would I be well?

I could think of no solutions, of no person safe to ask advice. I was in a trap, and the dark cloud squeezed all meaning in life from me. My mood was darker than those black outfits the Londoners wrapped themselves in.

"Come, Del, we're back at the hospital. You'll feel better in a while." Sister Marian sounded unconvinced.

# 33: To see me

I never saw Sister Marian again, but looked to another shining thread, Sister Carol, who went beyond a professional manner, cared from the heart, and appeared refreshed every shift. "We've had a meeting about you, Sister Della. The doctor wants to try electric shock treatment. He thinks you're depressed from service at the front, and the treatment will snap you back to your old self."

Some doctors viewed shock treatment as the latest thing, and they didn't want to be left behind. Later, shock treatment went in and out of fashion, mostly out. Eventually, the treatment was determined beneficial in particular cases.

"I don't want shock treatment, Sister. I've seen the convulsions, memory loss."

"Glad you feel that way, because I don't think it's called for in your case and I stood up to him for you. I think your work, poor nutrition in France, and then the Spanish influenza have given you physical and mental fatigue."

"Thank you, Sister Carol."

"But we have to get you eating."

"I know the food's good here, but it tastes awful to me. I want to throw up when I smell the meat. It must be my body just now, because I enjoyed everything before."

"What do you feel like eating?"

"I'd enjoy a dish made with potatoes, apples, and butter. At home we call it heaven and earth. I know butter's hard to get, but sometimes Cook does magic."

"I think she'd be happy to make it for you, Sister Della. What are the proportions?"

"Exact amounts don't matter, but I'd say for a pound and half of potatoes, add two apples. Chop it all up and boil the lot in salted water. Drain the pot well, then mash the potatoes and apples together with a good sized knob of butter, and add black pepper, and maybe a bit of salt. That's how we made it at home, though some people get fancy and top it with fried onions and bacon. I like it without the toppings. Butter, real butter, is important, and I do love black pepper."

"Cook'll make it delicious, I'm sure. Besides good food, you need rest and light activities. We're so short-staffed, it'd be wonderful if you could help with a few duties here."

"I'd like to return to nursing, but why would they want me back like this?"

"The way things are going on the Continent, with fierce battles and the Spanish influenza, the brass will send you to France again, whether you're recovered on not, so let's get you built up. How about we start with a little mending? Needle work should be soothing for you, and God knows, we can use the help."

Sister Carol brought me a few lisle stockings with holes, floss, and a needle, and I started immediately. My hands shook when I tried to thread the needle or aim it for a stitch.

"Maybe mending's not best for you right now. Take a rest and later we can try another task."

She came back with a trolley of clean equipment, small items. "Sister Della, our aides have more than they can do, so if you put these things away, it'd be a real help. You know how to handle things properly and understand it's important for them to be stored in the correct spot."

"I'd love to help, Sister Carol."

"Be sure to rest if you tire."

My physical and mental energy increased at a slow rate. Sister Carol added to the tasks: a greater number of items to shelve, and then bigger equipment. She invited me to take temperatures, and bathe patients, and then she began asking my opinion about suitable diets and techniques. She listened and adopted some of my suggestions.

"You're right, Sister Della. If you distract the patient and carefully slip in a needle, often the patient feels nothing."

By mid October, I was nursing most of the day. The hospital was experiencing so many absent nurses due to influenza, no one in administration or the nursing staff complained that I wasn't officially hired. The power of the dark cloud had mostly lifted so I took daily walks in the gardens and to the hospital library.

I started a novel by Briget Maclagan. The author described India of the early twentieth century, and I was daydreaming about travelling there when a letter arrived. I never finished the novel.

The letter, dated late in October 1918, was from the War Office and began:

> *I am directed to request that ...,*

and ordered me back to France.

*Can I nurse over there again? It's hell—the hours; the exhaustion! Rewarding, though. Maybe I can find out what happened to Charlie. I've lost weight, but if I'm pregnant, it'll show soon even if I'm skinny.*

An orderly announced that Matron Best wished to see me.

**Marie Mossman**

# 34: Obvious reasons

"Sister Della, you've received a letter from our Matron-in-Chief, who requests you return to duty with the British Armies in France?"

"Yes, Matron Best."

"I have confidence you're ready to resume work in France, if one can ever be prepared for the situation over there." She relaxed her tone. "I've reviewed the progress notes on your case and see that when you first arrived here, you were fevered and in a state of delirium, during which you produced a violent but short-lived menses. Be assured, we don't record a patient's comments during her delirium, unless they provide information helpful to the war cause. Your statements were not recorded. You'll leave here with an excellent report due to your behaviour and contributions to our hospital....Sister Della, we live during a war. We all do things we wouldn't in normal times. You're kind to others. Be kind and forgiving to yourself."

She inhaled and exhaled a deep breath. "You may go to Administration and complete hospital discharge formalities. I wish you well."

I could stop worrying about pregnancy!

It would be scary to leave the safety of the hospital, but I'd come over to help the war cause, and the greatest need was on the Continent. I straightened up, told myself to do what needed to be done.

"Matron Best, thank you for your kindness. I hesitate to ask, but could you possibly pass on my appreciation to Sister Marian, who has been especially compassionate while I've been here? I haven't seen her of late."

Matron Best looked down. She sighed. "I'm afraid Sister Marian was a victim of Spanish flu. We keep it quiet when we lose nurses, for obvious reasons."

My chest and abdominal muscles slumped at the news of Sister Marian's death.

"Do take care of yourself on the Continent," Matron said. Then she stood and offered her hand.

I wrote a note to Katherine to send on to my brother Dan, my closest family link in Nova Scotia. I assured him of my good health and eagerness to resume nursing in France. I expressed appreciation to Sister Carol and other nurses who had helped me recover, and said good-bye to them, and to my fellow patients at the hospital.

On my way to Administration, I fixed the image this hospital's clean, tidy wards in my brain as a reminder of sanity and kindness.

I enjoyed the tedious bureaucracy of formal discharge, and my mind raced toward France.

A red double-decker omnibus carried me, my bags, and my railway warrant through the streets of London to the train station. Little did it matter that the air was raw from a heavy rain. Too soon, the female conductor announced St. Pancras.

The station remained magnificent and functioned normally, but roof damage from bombing earlier in the year wasn't completely repaired.

They processed my travel warrant and I joined the crowd, mostly soldiers, who were funnelling into train cars. My QA uniform ensured respect from men, and a seat.

A young nurse joined me. "Hello, mind if I take the place beside you?" *English accent.*

"Do sit down. I'd like company."

"Canadian, are you? Been to Folkestone before?"

"Passed through once, but I didn't see anything. It was dark and hurried. I am Canadian, but was working in the States, so signed up with the American Red Cross."

"There's lots going on in Folkestone. People from all over. Masses of Canadians everywhere. Might see someone you know. Lots of dances and tea parties, but you have to take your own sugar. We've knitting and sewing circles. Always something useful to do, volunteering."

*That's why I'm going back.*

"I love the dances. The Canadian lads are good looking, strong chaps, always popular. Lots of girls aim to marry one, go off to Canada after the war. Not me, though, I'll stick it out here. It'll be grim for a while, but it'll get better, and my kids, if I ever have 'em, will be true English. You got a beau?"

"Yes, but we've lost contact since I was transported out of France."

"Happens a lot. Losing contact, I mean."

"Do you work in Folkestone?"

"At Victoria Hospital. Our Matron Browne was mentioned in *The Times* last year for her exceptional service. We've fifty-seven hospitals in the area. You could have your pick of a job, if you wanted. Why don't you stop with us a while?"

*We're not supposed to discuss plans with strangers.*

"I'll think about it."

"Well, if you go down to the dock, there's a tea room, the Harbour Canteen, run by volunteers. Everything's free. They keep a guest book for anyone passing through—into their seventh book. Have a look. You might see someone you know, your beau, even! And if you sign the book, he might spot your name. They say Churchill signed when he was there! We've made the turn, coming into Folkestone now. If you'd change your mind and come with me to the hospital, I'd introduce you to Matron. You could have a job on the spot."

"Thank you, Sister, but I think I'll go to the Harbour Canteen and look for my friend's name. A wonderful suggestion."

Marie Mossman

# 35: About her

The scene at Harbour Canteen was like a popular church pie sale. I sidled my way through the crowd of anxious men and women until I spied the guest books. There was a pile of closed books, and one book open to a page partially filled with signatures.

Impossible to find Charlie's signature before I board, unless he passed through recently.

I started with the latest signature and worked backward. He was proud of his penmanship, so I skipped over the illegible ones.

My heart leapt toward my throat when I saw the name *Geoffrey S--, July 1918*! I'd heard he was wounded in France, but nothing else. I sent a prayer skyward.

The coffee smelled delicious and most of the troops took sweets at the first opportunity, but I focused on scanning the endless list of signatures. Snippets of conversation pierced my concentration:

"Are we going on the *Princess Victoria*?"

"She had a near miss early on. Been lucky since our air surveillance got going."

"Think they'll wait 'til night?"

"Never tell us nothing."

I kept my eyes on the guest book pages until an announcement. "All QAs report immediately to the embarkation quay."

I signed and dated the next line on the visitor book: *Sister Della, Q.A.I.M.N.S.R.* Then I grabbed my bag.

"Sister, I noticed you've been busy. Have this hot drink 'fore you go. I can get another."

My eyes became teary. "Thank you, Captain."

I rushed to the line of nurses and crossed the ramp, not quite the last to board the troopship *Princess Victoria*.

We crossed the Channel in daylight, escorted by two destroyers. It was choppy, but nothing to bother me. U-boats left us in peace.

Another matter, however, caused excitement on the voyage. I'd noticed a friendly QA visiting with various nursing sisters. "Getting a bit chilly, isn't it?" she said, attempting to start a conversation with me. She smelled musty for a QA travelling from England to the Continent. We'd bathe properly when we had the chance.

"Not bad for October."

"I hope we safely cross."

*Something in her speech is odd.* "We will. Have to believe it."

"Where are you headed on the other side?"

*Maybe it's her voice?* "A hospital, I expect."

"Me too. I'm going to Etaples. Is it near where you'll be?"

"Not sure."

"There are a lot of troops moving. Wondering where they're all headed?"

*The shoulders of her uniform look too narrow for her body.* "Don't know."

"I think I'll walk a bit around, stay in the fresh air."

*That quirky speech again.*

She wandered off and approached another nursing sister.

There was something about this woman that made me uneasy. She struck up a conversation quickly, and if the other person gave short answers, she wandered on to another. When a person talked more, she remained to chat. Her walk was awkward.

I approached one of the ship's officers. "Sir, you see that QA over there? The one on the right, leaning on the rail? She asked me questions about where the troops were going, and there's something about her speech and uniform, and the way she moves, that makes me uneasy. Do you think she could be interviewed to check her out?"

"Can't be too cautious."

Shortly afterwards I spotted a ship's officer walking with the QA sister toward the bridge, and a couple of strong sailors discretely walking close by.

I wandered the decks most of the crossing, breathing the damp Channel air and hoping to run into nurses whom I knew, but without luck.

Loud conversations between men revealed they were impatient for war to end, and disrespectful of their leaders and the wealthy class in England. I was shocked to learn a couple of "For Officers Only" signs had been removed from doors of nicer facilities on board. How could we win a war against Germany if we couldn't get on among ourselves?

Tea and sandwiches appeared about halfway across the Channel. My regular and civilized meals at the London hospital were already history. Gone.

I could clearly discern cliffs and trees of the French coast as the officer I'd spoken with earlier approached me. "Sister, thank you for your observations. You won't be seeing that person free on deck again."

What a choice: reporting a person who will be punished, maybe executed, or not reporting and enabling a spy to pass information to the Germans. No joy either way.

I later learned she was a he and his luggage contained other disguises, and notes that would have been useful to the Germans.

The sea began to smell of oil and smoke, and shortly afterwards the announcement blared, "Prepare to disembark."

My order was to rejoin the British Armies in France. *Will I be met? Will there be transportation? Be strong for whatever comes.*

# 36: Frequent moves

Logistics were less chaotic than the first time I arrived in France. This time, from the gangplank, I saw a sign with my name, and another for Sister Karen. Karen from Ohio who had shared my cabin on the *Olympic* months ago! I remembered her negative attitude to lectures.

*Was it only months?*

Karen's thin face burst into a broad smile when she recognized me. "Sister Della! What have they done to you!"

I could have said the same to her. "We're still alive, Karen. Where've you been working?"

"We must catch up, but first I have to tell you, you were right. I've often wished I'd paid attention to those lectures on the *Olympic.*"

We sat together on the train. "Where've you been?" she asked.

"They sent me to a hospital in England first, to learn British nursing. Honestly, it was like learning a new language. And the food!"

"I know what you mean! Tea coming out of your pores, but a decent cup of coffee? Not in the country. The matrons know how to work you, though. I thought it was bad in training, back in the States."

"Where were you sent?"I asked.

"A hospital over here, early July. We worked with the Brits, refurbishing buildings, setting up new equipment, storing meds. Eighteen-hour days. Matron said I looked run down, sent me back to Blighty for a week of leave. Don't have a clue what to expect now."

"Keep faith the brass know what they're doing."

"Right." She nodded as she spoke. We both raised our eyebrows and held our lips tightly closed. Our eyes expressed an opinion we dared not utter, and we remained quiet the last miles to our station.

~

Matron welcomed Sister Karen and me on our arrival at #12 General Hospital. "Ladies, welcome back to active service in France. Recently we've lost several nurses to this dreadful Spanish influenza, so we're truly in need of you. Fortunately, of late we've received fewer wounded soldiers, and we've adopted more appropriate practices for handling influenza patients, so we manage the cases better. You may go directly from here to mess if you need a meal, then rest in your room this evening. I'll call you individually in the morning for your instructions. Sister Karen, good evening. Sister Della, I'll have a word with you before you go."

Sister Karen's footsteps receded far down the wooden corridor before Matron continued. "Sister Della, correspondence has accumulated for you during your absence. A massive envelope arrived shortly after your evacuation to England. I expected your return, hoped for it, I must say, and so let the letters pile up."

She handed me a thick eight by eleven inch envelope and several personal letters of normal size. "I couldn't help noticing all the letters on army stationery are addressed by the same hand. Someone must care a lot for you." She sighed, then continued, "Good evening, Sister Della. We'll discuss your posting in the morning."

I hurried directly to my room, a canvas cubicle. I noted an antiseptic smell. Otherwise, it was just as I'd left it several weeks ago.

I opened the manila envelope and read.

> *My Dearest Della,*
>
> *I have married you by proxy. A kind (Is there any other sort?) nurse stood in for you. As you see, the ceremony was witnessed by my commanding officer and a friend from the Nova Scotia Highlanders. You should find four signed copies of the marriage document in this envelope. You and a witness are to add your signatures to each copy and you are each to keep a copy. Return the others to me. One will be stored in my breast pocket and one will be held by my trusted commanding officer, because the brass may look for proof of his attestation in future.*
>
> *This is the best we can do at this time. When we are together again, we can repeat our vows. I urge you to complete your signing immediately to ensure our status.*
>
> *My Dearest, fortified with your love I feel I could conquer the whole German army single handed. Sincerely, Charlie*

I looked at the papers and cried. Dear Charlie, he truly believed he could work magic. He had done his utmost to establish our marriage, but I knew the proxy arrangement was like leaning over a cliff. The American and Canadian bureaucracies would use their power to push us into the pits below instead of recognizing our marriage.

I did love Charlie and knew his actions were sincere, so I decided to complete the documents at my earliest break, which might or might not be the next day. I sorted Charlie's letters by date and slathered myself with his sweet words until his last note:

> *Dear Della,*
> *They are sending me to hospital in Etaples to recover from a sickness. Will be in touch as soon as possible.*
> *Sincerely,*
> *Charlie*

*Spanish influenza? An infection? They don't send you to hospital for a minor problem.*

Sleep evaded me for hours, but discipline woke me early morning.

I knocked on Matron's door.

"Come in, Sister Della. True to your reputation, on time to the minute."

"I try, Matron. Am I to resume duty in the wards today?"

"Staffing requirements have changed. We need you elsewhere. You're to join a new Surgical Team at a CCS. It requires an experienced and superior senior nurse. Your recommendation came from higher up, and I'm in complete agreement with it. As you know, only our top nurses are assigned to these teams. Do you feel up to the strenuous physical demands? It'll be more dangerous than ward work here. You understand the conditions from your previous experiences."

"Of course, Matron. Could you tell me where I'll be sent?"

"Expect frequent moves. I can inform you no further."

"I'd like to take the posting, no question. When will I join the team?"

"We'll give you a day or so to acclimatize here, filling in shifts, and between times you're to gather your necessary materials. I expect Dr. Ernst to pass through any day, pick you up and brief you during your drive to the front. So you're on board?"

"Definitely, Matron."

"I'll include our meeting in today's report to Chief Nurse Stimson. You may attend to your personal matters and preparations this morning. I've scheduled you for a shift, beginning at fifteen hundred hours." She was being unusually generous in the free time she granted me.

*Why did she mention my personal matters? Stop fretting. Focus on what needs to be done.*

I approached the padre to witness my signature.

"Sister Della, I won't pry into your reasons for this arrangement, but you do realize if word gets out you're married, your matron will pose incisive questions about your behaviour and you may be faced with disciplinary action based solely on suspicion. This is possibly the greatest danger to you."

He waited for a reply. I bit my tongue rather than utter regrettable words.

After a moment, the padre continued. "Picture who might consider this document the basis for a claim for a widow's allowance, should Charlie be killed. If nothing else, they'll say the marriage was never consummated, or your behaviour was unacceptable before the proxy ceremony. You'll be threatened with a dishonourable discharge."

"There's nothing in the document that is untrue or dishonourable."

He gave me a long look. "You're in a vulnerable situation. I'm uncomfortable with you signing this document, but will be your witness and keep this matter between you and me as long as you wish, or at least as long as I can."

I married Charles Rafuse in a secretive, shameful, clandestine manner. We had no hope of leave in the near future. All this transpired during my first thirty-six hours at the hospital.

Fortunately, I had little to pack for my drive with Dr. Ernst.

# 37: I like you

Forty-eight hours after my arrival at #12 General, I sat next to Dr. Ernst as he drove us in a truck toward routine life and death experiences close to the Front.

"Sister Della, have you ever run a Dangle Parade?" he asked almost as soon as we had set out.

"No. I've heard of them, but—"

"That's what I suspected. I've requested you drive with me to our station so I can fill you in on my expectations, and so you'd be captured, I mean committed, and couldn't change your mind."

I liked him already. He had a sense of humour.

Dr. Ernst resembled a cousin of mine who had lived rough as a cowboy on the plains of Montana and later homesteaded in Saskatchewan. They both had a strong jaw, full lips, a straight nose, lively eyes and a broad forehead with retreating hairline. Ernst was of medium height. His uniform failed to hide his muscles. Similar looks, but would Ernst have my cousin's survival grit?

I remembered Matron telling me that around Philadelphia he was an esteemed orthopaedic surgeon, crude as the rest when operating, but he could turn on the charm.

Dr. Ernst had been quietly gracious when she introduced me to him. Now he drove like an eel escaping the hook. We flew along a bumpy road, direction Cambrai. However, I heard his voice easily above the rattles and squeaks of our Ford as we drove northeast.

"Syphilis and other venereal diseases, we call them all VD, are infecting our soldiers at an astounding rate. We'll have a generation of children with reduced intelligence, blindness and physical malformations, if this goes on."

"So we'll run a Dangle Parade?"

"You're quick, but make that plural."

"How many?"

"The men'll line up every week, trousers open, penis and scrotum hanging out. You'll check each one for a lesion."

"And then?"

"You'll order any soldier with the tiniest sign of VD to stand aside. I'll triage those cases."

"How so?"

"I'll ship the advanced ones directly to our venereal hospital in Etaples. We'll treat the nascent cases immediately."

I wondered which hospital in Etaples specialized in VD. They had sent Charlie to Etaples. I forced my voice to sound calm and professional, asking, "What's the latest treatment for early syphilis?"

"We irrigate the urethra with antiseptic and apply Calomel Ointment externally."

I wondered if Ernst was planning to be half of the 'we'. "I've heard men call the ointment pinky panky."

"You're up to date, Sister. Earlier on, the fighting was so constant that we held dangles erratically, if you pardon the phrase. But our side's making progress, so, with you on board, I'm planning a weekly routine."

"I'll do my best to save the next generation."

Dr Ernst laughed. "I like you, Sister. You have a sense of humour. Thought you mightn't."

We drove on in silence for a bit, and when he next spoke, his tone was serious. "Sister, you mustn't judge these men harshly. We're fighting a war, and sex bolsters their morale. Reality is, intercourse takes place. Men seek it. Local women are so starved they'll do anything for a meal or money to buy food for their children. And so VD proliferates."

"You're broad minded, Dr. Ernst."

"Helps with the digestion. Seriously, I advise you to take precautions before you hop in bed with any eager male. Unnecessary advice in your case, as I presume your behaviour's exemplary."

"Where do we meet the rest of our team?"

"They're already at our CCS. We're replacing their doctor and nurse, who died recently. You and I were unassigned, you, because you just returned from leave. Me, because I'm the lone survivor of....of my team."

He gripped the wheel tightly, slowed speed. His eyes became moist, and his facial muscles tightened.

I heard only the noises of the car, until I managed, "I'm sorry."

"Did I mention we're at war? Three wars, actually, and the Germans are the least of it."

"Three?"

"I told you about treating the men for VD. We have to get them cleaned up before they're shipped home. You know about the Huns already. Worst of all is this Spanish influenza. We're losing the most men and women to flu! Can you believe it? Flu!"

"I can. It's epidemic in London."

"That brings me to the second reason we've been chosen. They think we may be immune. I haven't caught the flu, and you've survived it."

"Okay."

"There's one more reason."

"Oh?"

"We're damned good. Don't you forget it."

My shoulders relaxed and I smiled spontaneously before asking how we were for supplies.

"That's why we're in a truck. We have gallons of antiseptic and ointment for the dangles. No man'll leave our parade unserviced. Not the service he prefers, but the one he needs."

I was less embarrassed by his next topic. "The flu cases are tricky because we don't have much to treat them. Only masks and aprons to protect ourselves, lots of linen ordered, detergent and antiseptic for cleaning. We isolate the cases as best we can and ship them to a hospital on the first transportation available."

He glanced at me, then looked back at the road and jerked the wheel to keep us out of the ditch. "Enough shop talk for now. They say you're strictly straight-laced. Tell me, do you have a beau, Sister?"

"It's complicated."

"Often is. I won't pry, but see these shoulders. They're strong if you need something to lean on."

"Thank you. I appreciate it. And you, Dr. Ernst, do you have a family?"

"Yes, my wife and two sons. it was hard to leave them in Philadelphia. I hope to God he doesn't, but my first son might enlist after his birthday. Sounds hokey, I know, but I'm here because I believe every soldier deserves the treatment I'd want for him."

The cloudy sky ahead of us shimmered and appeared to ripple. "Did you see that?" I said, trying to keep my voice calmer than my heartbeat.

"The fireworks? The last CCS got too close to them. We'll be further back from the shooting. The brass have learned it's handy to keep us medics alive."

"Can you tell me now where we'll set up?"

"We'll stay southwest of Cambrai. The Brits and Canadians'll bring casualties to us, over the Canal du Nord. Expect a backlog when we get there."

"What do we have on board for operating supplies?"

"We have regular splints, drips, bandages, cleaning supplies, and enough morphine in the back to keep us happy for days. Regular shipments should come through at this stage."

"Any contingency arrangements if shipments are interrupted?"

"If things get really rough, I've got a bottle or two of whisky to help me along. You're welcome to share, if you're inclined."

"Generally I take tea."

"Too bad."

We jounced along for a few more miles, then he said. "We're operating more than we used to at casualty clearing stations, as the Brits like us to call them. Better results if we treat the boys early. Your operating room skills'll come in handy."

"You've had a detailed report on me."

"Only the parts they thought pertained to our work, Sister. All your secrets are safe."

*How, then, does he know I have secrets?*

"Mustn't take it personally if I get rude at times. It happens when you're losing the battle for a fella's life."

"I understand, doctor. I'll try to match your dedication."

He snorted, an appreciative laugh, then said. "This road coming up on our right'll be our last turn. Brace yourself."

# 38: I'll swear

"Here's home, our CCS site. It's you, me, and an orderly––if we're lucky, Sister. You can add a company or two of soldiers, but our station ain't no London General."

There were tents on platforms and a network of wooden walkways to join them and keep us out of the mud. Dozens of injured lay on cots near our tents. Able-bodied men were setting up camp essentials: a sanitation centre, a mess tent, and more walkways. The land looked trampled and rutted by the armies' recent advances and retreats

The sergeant and another officer strode toward us, as we climbed out of our truck. Sarge, a tall,  large-boned man, introduced himself and his medical officer, a wiry looking fellow.

Sarge nodded to a small group nearby and shouted, "Men, unload the doc's truck and set his supplies up as he orders." Then he turned back to Dr. Ernst.

Dr. Ernst handed me his medical supply list for re-ordering, I interpreted his writing for the medical officer, where necessary, so the officer could relay the order. I then supervised placement of my supplies, and Ernst set up his office area.

He rubbed his hands together with enthusiasm, once the basics were in place. "We're to treat men before they're transported to the 1000-bed hospital further west. We can start shortly, Sister."

It suited me. I could hear and feel the looming power of battle not far to the east. Getting to work operating would keep me from dwelling on the danger.

"Have you sent the order for replacement supplies?" Ernst asked.

"Yes, sir. I've confirmed with our medical officer, enough to keep us ahead of need, if everything comes as requested."

We had no time for a Dangle Parade the first days after our arrival because of the surgery backlog and constant additions to it. There was barely time to breathe between one patient and the next.

I learned immediately one approach that turned on Dr. Ernst's nasty. "Should I sterilize the guillotine?" It was often employed in mass amputation situations.

A flurry of expletives shot my way, concluding with,"NO! I won't use that butcher's tool! I'll amputate in a proper manner. Keep the line moving."

Our orderly, Henri, brought in the next wounded soldier. Our patient appeared less than sixteen years of age.

"I didn't think it would happen," he whimpered.

I administered an injection of morphine, and set up the Dakin's drip to flush the wound.

Dr. Ernst's cutting was precise and rapid. I administered anaesthetics, adjusted the tourniquet, blotted blood, handed him instruments when he needed them. His work was consistent with the latest recommendations I'd read in *Surgery at a Casualty Clearing Station*.

He positioned skin flaps to reduce risk of adhesion problems. He took care to protect nerve ends, to reduce pain. Dr. Ernst operated skilfully in the time a less-talented or less-committed medic might need to use a guillotine. His fine amputations would facilitate fitting of a modern artificial leg to the stump.

"Henri, remove this soldier to the recuperation area and bring the next case," I ordered.

Ernst and I moved like a team of carriage horses during surgeries. We had trained under similar systems in the northeastern states, so understood and followed the same routines and used the same medical terminology.

We finished eighteen hours of surgery the first day. I was exhausted and exhilarated. Ernst was in a positive mood more often than not, and he gave credit to me and Henri, as if our support enabled his achievement.

Henri, a French peasant, might have been 50 or 80, yet he willingly carried stretcher cases. He never complained, always looked exhausted, and responded immediately to orders.

"Sister, I do this work for my son," he explained to me. "The Germans killed him near St. Pierre, where my family farmed in peace until this senseless war. My son's image gets me up when you call. He walks beside me when I carry a stretcher. He may not be real, but he provides me with strength."

"I'm sorry for your loss," was all I could say.

"Sister Della enables me to operate at top efficiency," I overheard Dr. Ernst say to our sergeant one day, deflecting the officer's praise. "She's a perfectionist in cleanliness, and organization, and has exercised foresight in ordering our materials."

We operated steadily for a couple days until our side launched a major assault. We heard firing from large calibre guns once fierce fighting started. The ground shook from shells exploding. Shrapnel tore holes in our surgery tent as we worked.

We received orders one night to evacuate patients and ourselves to Quéant, the closest large medical centre. Ernst had me cramming precious equipment into crates and Henri lining up our hundred or so stretcher cases for transport by truck or horse cart.

"You and Henri go, Della. Fuck the order. I'm staying to treat wounded men who make it here."

"Dr. Ernst, I'm staying to assist you, sir," I said. My tone was sharp, like cut crystal.

"I order you to go with Henri, Sister."

"And I'll swear you disobeyed the brass's order to leave. I'm staying to assist you."

He looked me straight on. His shoulders slumped and he let out a forceful sigh. "Damn it. You're tough as oak. Okay. Help Henri get off. We'll operate on the next casualty after he's on his way."

"Yes sir." Strength ran through my body.

Henri and our patients were about to leave in convoy for Quéant, when an officer arrived. "We've got the Germans retreating. The brass have rescinded the evacuation order."

Ernst looked from the officer to the evacuation convoy, and back to the officer. "Hell. Now we have to unload them."

To me, more quietly, he said. "Thank you, Sister, for sticking with me. I'll never forget it."

His sincere tone sent shivers through my shoulders. I replied. "Just my duty, sir."

Ernst and I later received medals for bravery under fire at Cambrai, which united us in a conspiracy of secrecy about our intended refusal to follow orders.

The Allies' continuing success created a quiet period, so Ernst finally had a chance to order a Dangle Parade, to be followed by a surprise. I would have to get myself and the men through our parade first, though.

"The sergeant will order the men to line up, expose the genital area, stand straight and look ahead," Ernst said. "He'll instruct the men not to speak to you, except to reply properly if you send them to me for further investigation. Inspect the sergeant first. Check the genitals and surrounding area for warts, rashes, lesions, mucous, bumps, or any other exceptionality. If you see anything, send the man to me."

I rearranged his list of signs into a mnemonic: *war limb* (warty area rashes, inspect lesions, mucous, bumps) for easy remembering until the inspections became routine.

"And the men who are clean?"

"That's our surprise. After the men are cleared, they'll follow Sarge to the field behind us, where the boys'll organize a ball game. Work smartly, Sister, 'cause when we're finished inspection, we get to watch the game."

"May I use a pair of our rubber gloves, Doctor?"

He hesitated, but then the muscles around his eyes relaxed, and his face appeared less hardened. "Of course, Sister."

Everyone cooperated. Who wanted to miss the game?

An enormous boom came from beyond the Bourlon Woods, east of the canal. The sergeant flinched. The men's faces fell. A grindstone dropped on my spirits. Would the ballgame be cancelled? But a general barrage did not follow the first explosion.

I inspected 300 men in the afternoon and referred 48 of them to Dr. Ernst. He ordered me to administer treatment to 30 men, with the aid of Henri. Ernst sent the other 18 on their way to Etaples for extensive treatment. Rumour had it VD cases in Etaples had to empty bedpans, collect garbage, and mop vomit. I felt sorry for the 18, but not for long.

The sergeant's voice boomed. "Carry on, men. Play ball!"

Soldiers smoothed bumps in the terrain and laid out the field, marking the three bases and home plate. Corporals formed their men into teams. A bat, ball and gloves appeared from from a tent.

The sergeant announced a British style game, with extra outfielders, and that he would umpire.

The men ran and shouted themselves warm on this October day. I winced to see the scrapes on some of the boys from sliding into a base or falling on rocks, but no one came looking for a bandage.

The score was close late in the last game, with both teams composed of Canadians and British men. The pitcher delivered a fastball, underhand, with minimum spin. The batter blasted the gift straight back. The ball struck the pitcher's forehead, dead centre. The pitcher lay flat on his back. Game over.

"Dr. Ernst!"

Ernst walked across the field to check the pitcher, who was already struggling up, his corporal nearby. Ernst turned to the corporal. "Excuse this man from demanding duties for the remainder of the day. Bring him to me if he vomits."

The sergeant ordered silence. "Officially we have a tied game. Congratulations, men, well played. Stand easy. Corporals, form your men by company. Companies, line up alphabetically for chow. See to it. This'll be a welcome change from trench rations."

"Sister, I've ordered meals brought to our station," Dr. Ernst, said.

"May I ask if there's another parade planned for next week?"

"There will be, if we're still here."

# Marie Mossman

# 39: No lights

I slept fitfully. Nova Scotia Highlanders were scheduled for Dangle Parade the next morning. How could I suss out information on Charlie with the men commanded not to speak to me, except to say, "Yes, Sister," when I directed them to do something? Another awkward aspect was the probability of inspection of a man I recognized!

A company of Highlanders marched into camp early in the morning, and a sergeant approached us. "Dr. Ernst, I'm relaying an order to dismantle this CCS for transportation."

"From whom? I've not been informed of a move."

"Perhaps you'll receive the order momentarily, sir."

A runner appeared as the sergeant spoke. Dr. Ernst scanned the order, then turned to me. "Sister Della, pack our supplies. Transportation'll arrive shortly for our new site. No, I don't know where the hell it'll be!"

He ordered Henri to line up our patients for transport to our hospital at Quéant.

I sang to myself. "Jingle jangle, no dangle."

I packed our precious surgical gloves, Dakin's drip kits, bottles of antiseptic, morphine, bandages, the items important to a nurse for surgical procedures, or fragile for transportation. Dr. Ernst assembled the tools most useful to him.

"I don't like leaving the rest of the packing to soldiers."

"Leave it, Sister, 'cause we're ordered out before them. We're to set up closer to new action."

Soldiers loaded the most important crates into our ambulance, and Dr. Ernst drove us away from our Cambrai site.

"We aren't the first to run away from Cambrai's ruins. Armies have taken what they wanted and marched out of here since Roman times. Will it ever change?"

"Can you tell me where we're going?"

"No. Let's be cheerful, Sister Della."

We drove on in silence for a few kilometres, until he cleared his throat and said. "Sister, I continue to appreciate how you joined me when the order to evacuate was, uh, unclear, back in Cambrai. Why did you do it?"

"Loyalty, I suppose," I said. "I agree with your determination to give the best possible treatment to our soldiers, and I admire your skill, so I like assisting you in surgery. I'm here to nurse anywhere care is needed."

I didn't add that I enjoyed being around him. He was vibrant, and physically attractive.

"Explanation accepted, but only if you let me return it double. You're one solid woman, Della."

I blushed and could think of no suitable response.

Later I saw a road sign for Rumilley-Cambrésis. "Are we retreating?"

"Not exactly. I rushed us out of there because I want to take a detour. There's a decent restaurant off this road. We may as well have a good lunch before we're back in the fray," he said.

My body leaned left as he turned onto a curvy side road. I saw a group of bushes in front of a stand of spruce. The last swerve revealed a shabby building with a damaged sign '**staurant' hanging slantwise above the entrance.

He opened his door. "Come on. It's on me."

I remembered my weekend with Charlie and put myself on guard.

The scent of fresh baking and clatter of pots met us at the door. The dining room invited us with its tablecloths and service plates waiting. The host greeted us, chatted in French with me a bit about the cold, foggy weather, and then led us to a table by the hearth where he recited the menu choices.

"Madame, you will take?"

"Could you possibly tell me what *zander* is?"

"It's fish, a kind of perch that we catch in rivers. We serve it with fig sauce."

"That is tempting, but I'll have your white bean soup, Picardy style crêpes, and a macaroon with coffee, please."

"Sir?"

"The duck pâté, leek pie, and do you have a cake? You didn't mention one."

"I regret we don't have enough eggs for our special cake"

"Then, I'll have a macaroon with coffee, and bring a glass of white wine with the pie, please."

"Certainly, sir."

The soup warmed me and soothed my stomach.

Ernst invited me to try his pâté, but I didn't want to share food, so refused.

"Good, I was hoping you'd let me have it all. Della, if I may drop the Sister when we're off duty, where did you learn French?"

"We had reading and writing it in the higher grades, and then I taught French myself for ten years when I was a teacher. I understand restaurant language, anyway."

"You speak enough to impress me. And I didn't know you were a teacher."

My eyebrows raised themselves slightly and a tiny smile played at the corners of my mouth. "Matron didn't tell you everything?"

My rolled crêpes arrived. They were topped with melted cheese and tasted divine. "How's your pie?" I asked between mouthfuls.

"Beats rations by a mile. I want to take French cooks home after the war and settle them in restaurants around Philly."

"I notice you keep a lamp on in the evenings. Is it to ward off evil spirits?" I asked.

"After my whisky, which I'm still hoping you'll share with me, reading calms my mind and brings on sleep. Cheaper than opiates."

The host came to our table. "Do you wish your coffee after your macaroon?"

"At the same time, please. The Sister and I must continue our trip shortly."

Dr. Ernst repeated his escaping eel performance as we sped away from the restaurant, in the direction of Cambrai. "After a bit, we'll turn on the road to our new site."

"Can you tell me *now* where we're going?"

"You'll know when we arrive. If we're captured en route, and you're interrogated, you have no information useful to the enemy."

~

"Damn, the fog has lifted," Dr Ernst said as he skidded the ambulance to a halt.

I wondered what was wrong with clear weather.

We were looking at a hillock, crested by dense shrubs. The flat terrain in our immediate area was tinted yellow and brown. In the distance, we could see a ridge.

"We'll stay behind the hill until dusk," Ernst said.

Trucks with unlit lights arrived later. Soldiers hopped out and erected a tent. The men were unusually quiet.

"We'll need light to set up our areas inside the tents," I said.

"Orders are, 'no lights, no noise.' As before, we're to concentrate on orthopaedic surgery and Dangle Parades. We'll direct other cases to transportation. Sister, organize the surgery and other areas in the morning. Sleep, if you can find a cot."

I did.

Next morning I heard, "Men, line up for Dangle Parade. You know what to show. Stand easy until the doctor and sister inspect you. Look straight ahead, and don't speak unless spoken to."

Fortunately, our parade materials were crated, in our vehicle, and accessible. No one mentioned a party following this Dangle Parade, so I took comfort in my memory of the previous day's restaurant lunch with Ernst.

The sergeant went first in line, like the last time. He announced. "Lance corporals, when your men are finished here, band members are to fall in with their leader. They're to warm up on regular songs everyone knows. Organize the other men to drill until our concert begins. Work them hard 'cause we've ordered good grub today."

I donned a pair of gloves and started checking genitals. The men looked as humiliated as before, but I found the process less embarrassing this time, until some of the soldiers looked familiar.

One company was from the Nova Scotia 85th Highlander Regiment. I hoped I wouldn't have to send any of them to Dr. Ernst.

Again, we inspected about 300 men. This time, Ernst had to re-check 45 soldiers and gave 15 men slips for Etaples. I had to treat 30 others.

I noted the numbers were consistent with the last site and took comfort from the knowledge that our embarrassing parades would help keep families back home healthy.

As the soldiers marched off, one nudged another. I overheard, "Charlie's woman." I froze.

The lance corporal barked, "Give me fifty!"

One particular soldier, a tall, strong man, had grown up along the coast where I did. He avoided looking at me. Dr. Ernst sent him to Etaples.

"What was going on last night, sir?"

"Surprise attack. Our boys crossed the Selle River, climbed a ladder to the ridge you saw in the distance, and pushed the Huns east. We're keeping up pressure and the Germans are fighting hard. The lads here'll be in battle tomorrow."

Dr. Ernst checked until the surgery area was as he wished. Once he had a table and his files, he attended to paperwork.

I heard the band tuning up and once it started playing popular songs, the soldiers spontaneously joined in, often substituting ribald lines for the original. The band and singing were so loud even I felt comfortable joining on "It's a Long Way to Tipperary" and "Pack up your Troubles in Your Old Kit-Bag and Smile, Smile, Smile".

Some rebel called for "Hanging on the Old Barbed Wire", but the band launched into "Mademoiselle from Armentières". Brass didn't like "Hanging on the Old Barbed Wire", because its lyrics mocked officers and pictured the ordinary soldier, dead, hanging from barbed wire. "Mademoiselle from Armentières" delivered morale-boosting thoughts of a lady lifting her skirts for male pleasure.

A crew arrived with the rest of our tents, so my attention turned to supervising Henri and a few privates as they unpacked our cots and other equipment for recuperating patients. Henri worked like an intelligent and faithful old horse. He made my job easy because he remembered how equipment had been arranged at our Cambrai site.

I was free to check supplies and ensure proper sanitation. Chow trucks drove up. Lance Corporals yelled for their men to form a line. The food smelled inviting across the field.

"Henri, see what you can get us," I said.

Sarge marched up to us. "You've heard, I presume, elements in Germany and Austria are pressing their governments to ask for armistice."

Ernst stood up from his desk and replied, "Might be a rumour. We don't need a weak agreement. We're advancing." His tone discouraged further discussion when he thanked the sergeant.

I saw another man walking in our direction. "Is this more trouble?"

Dr. Ernst looked up. "No. This gentleman is Dr. Jones, our anaesthetist."

I had not known we expected an anaesthetist and I wondered if his presence would affect my role in surgery.

He met Jones with a vigorous handshake and pat on the back. "You old rascal, you've made it! Delighted to have you on the team!" Then he turned the newcomer toward me. "Dr. Jones, meet our excellent nurse, Sister Della."

Jones said, "Sister, it's a pleasure." His eyes roamed over me in a leering manner.

"Dr. Jones, pleased to meet you, sir," I said. I shrivelled within myself, unable to confront his brazen stare.

"No need to look disappointed, Sister. Dr. Jones is as charming as I am during surgery. We learned the same bad manners in med school. There'll be plenty of work for the three of us."

I relaxed slightly after Dr. Ernst's assurance.

"Now we have a third, it'll be easier to use our Thomas knee splints," Ernst said. "Jones, I expect we'll be in surgery later today. I can't wait."

"They said they were sending me to a small CCS, but is this it?"

"This is it," Ernst and I replied together. To me, he said, "Sister, when you order splints, be sure to specify the bed-splint variety."

I wanted to get back to surgery, but would Jones act like a colleague, or treat me like a servant, as most doctors treated nurses? I wished I were a doctor. I was as smart as most of those I had met.

Dr. Jones, we have methadone. Do you wish me to order chloroform?"

"No, I use chloroform rarely. Ether is usually contraindicated as well. I administer nitrous oxide or a mix of it and oxygen when a general anaesthetic is required. I've brought supplies in my truck and have requested regular deliveries of the drugs I need, and will continue to do so."

I appreciated he could relieve pain in more ways than I could. Perhaps we three would make a better team than I had feared.

# 40: Into motion

"Look here, Jones," Dr. Ernst said, "we got this fellow shortly after the event. His tibia's in several pieces, not a good prognosis, but the bits are mostly attached to the periosteum. We're caught up on surgeries, so why don't we give him a chance to keep his leg?"

Jones shook his head and screamed a silent 'No!'

Ernst leaned over the pale man on the operating table. "Hey, soldier, you don't want a wooden leg, do you?"

"Uuuuuh."

"You'd like us to save yours, wouldn't you?"

"Uuuuh."

"Good choice."

"We'll have coffee instead of supper, and operate right away," Ernst said. "Sister, up his warming. We'll have Henri bring you a cuppa."

We'd completed countless surgeries after lunch, most of them life-saving amputations. It didn't look to me as though we could preserve this limb, but Dr. Ernst was in charge, so I padded our patient with warmed blankets, placed a warm bottle on his abdomen and new hot water bottles between his arms and rib cage.

I verified the primus stove was fuelled, ready to warm our patient during his long operation. He had already received an anti-tetanus injection, and intravenous solution to supplement his blood. I hoped our patient could not hear the intense whispers piercing the surgery room canvas walls.

"Ernst, think of the risks! This fellow's on the verge of shock as it is. You know how few in his shape pull through a long operation!" Jones said.

I readied the Dakin's drip, antiseptics, bandages, a Thomas knee splint, and surgery tools for Dr. Ernst.

Henri brought in a lukewarm coffee for me. I stood ready for the doctors.

"It's my decision, Jones, chop off his leg or take the risk. I'm operating."

"I'll record my objection."

"Your prerogative. Dope him, Jones."

"Yes, sir."

Jones returned to the operating tent and administered a minimal dose of morphine under the soldier's skin, then turned on our latest machinery which supported oxygen levels for patients.

~

"First, I'll align the bones close to their natural positions, then start to clean."

"Sister, stem the haemorrhaging! Warm him, damn it, his heart's racing!"

I tightened the tourniquet, then applied pressure at the haemorrhaging site with a wad of gauze. Jones left his post to grab more warm blankets for me to position around our patient. As soon as the blood leakage ebbed, I surrounded the soldier with new hot water bottles.

I used a soft voice. "It'll be all right. This doctor's the best. We want you to get better. Be strong. You're a brave man. The doctor must clean your leg and then he'll set your bones. We'll put a splint on so they heal properly. We're here with you."

I hung a new bottle of solution to replace his lost blood. His vital signs became more normal. Dr. Ernst worked a couple of hours to remove stray bone splinters and contaminated tissue, then he carefully aligned the long bone pieces and ensured that soft tissue was in place, too.

Finally, he and Dr. Jones secured the reconstructed leg in its splint.

"Jones, we deserve a whisky. Sister, you'll take a drink with us?"

"No, thank you."

"Then, Sister, you may retire, now."

"But Dr. Ernst––"

"You triage in the morning until we're about. It's an order. Go. Jones and I'll watch the lad."

I washed my hands and fell into my chilly bed, with my uniform on. I heard Ernst and Jones.

"What's with this cold fish nurse you've got?"

"She can't be as straight-laced as she puts on. She's hanging on hopes about some lecher's promise. Pity, isn't it?" Ernst spoke quietly.

"Yeah. Hmm."

"Remember that first weekend at med school?" Ernst spoke more loudly. "Someone rented a house and the idea was for all of us to get stinking drunk. Green, was it? Decided he'd developed flying powers and jumped from the second storey? Paid for it, lugging a cast on his leg the whole term."

"The religious fellow from Tennessee listened to the spicy jokes and fainted. Blamed it on the shocking stories."

"And the landlord's salamander scared Rob. He was the huskiest man in our year."

"So we had a giant stuffed salamander made for our class mascot. The frat guys burned their brains trying to figure out its meaning."

I got sleepier and heard no more, but was miserable. I missed the after-surgery collegial conversation with Ernst. I wanted to know where Charlie was and longed for his company.

Morning broke to a clear sky. A barrage of shelling sounded from over the hill, far away. Henri alternated between attending to recuperating patients and placing new ones. There were few of Henri's decisions to change when I triaged for surgery.

Jones and Ernst appeared shortly after I was up.

"Our last fellow had improving vitals when we turned in," Ernst said. "How's he this morning?"

"Appropriate signs. I administered morphine for his pain."

"Good."

We turned our attention to a soldier who complained of a severe headache, a sign of cerebral compression.

"Prep this one next," Ernst ordered.

I shaved and cleaned the skull. Jones injected the patient's drugs and monitored his state.

"I'll make a triangular incision to expose the wounded tissue."

I passed instruments to Dr. Ernst as needed. He used forceps and a baster-like instrument to remove foreign matter and damaged tissue from the wound, then he applied antiseptic. "This oily solution's the better choice," he said.

Ernst closed the skull and then brought skin flaps together to complete the operation.

I loved the rhythm of assisting at the surgery and enjoyed being part of the team again.

We took tea in the surgery afterwards. I sensed Jones leering at me.

"Do you have a beau, Sister?"

"Not really."

"What do you mean, 'Not really'?"

"Lay off her, Jones. Life's complicated. She's a prize nurse and I won't have her upset!"

"Understood." He raised his eyebrows, then lowered them and pursed his lips. "Nice job there, Ernst."

We received orders to move our CCS again. Ernst decided he and Jones would drive the ambulance filled with the most essential surgery supplies and equipment. Henri and I would follow in a truck, also loaded with materials. I'd be safe with dear grandfatherly Henri who had a farmer's ability to repair anything.

Ernst didn't trust Henri, however, to chauffeur me. I would drive.

"I've never learned how."

"No matter. Come on. I'll show you."

"It starts with the key, right?"

"Right. Turn the key, listen for the motor....Good girl."

*I'm not a girl, Ernst.*

"Left foot on the brake, right on the clutch, the middle pedal....Now, change the gear into low. Clutch in, let the clutch out slowly, then when you're ready, take your left foot off the brake and gently push your right foot on the accelerator to go forward....Super."

"And to stop?"

"Take your right foot off the accelerator and put your left on the brake."

"Got it!"

"Practise a bit around the yard. Remember, you must have the clutch in when you change gears."

"If I forget?"

"The truck's ruined and you get a dishonourable discharge. But it won't happen. Once you get the hang of starting and driving slowly, take a short run down the road to learn the higher gears. Della, we don't have time for you to learn properly. Concentrate like you do in surgery and you'll be okay."

He patted my shoulder. "I gotta get back to my reports. You'll do fine."

"What about the emergency brake?"

"It's not hilly around here."

"Sir, stopping in an emergency is important."

"Okay," he sighed. "If your regular brakes fail, take your foot *off* the G.D. accelerator pedal, and pull up with all your guts on this lever. 'K.? Get up to speed and give it a go now."

I didn't understand why such a fuss was made about driving being a special skill for men only. The basics weren't hard to learn.

"Thank you, Dr. Ernst, for your help. Can you tell me where we're heading?"

"When the time comes. Soon as you can handle the truck a bit, return to organize the boxes that go in the ambulance."

Ernst told me directions to a village where we were to set up our CCS, and he gave me a rough sketch of the route at the last minute.

"If you lose sight of our ambulance, you're to continue to the church in that village. We'll have our dorm tent erected tonight and establish the surgery in the morning."

Henri and I headed to the Ypres area in Flanders. Ernst tore off, presumably in the direction of Ypres.

I jerked our half of the convoy into motion and followed Ernst's muddy tire tracks for some miles until I met an intersection where it was impossible to ascertain whether he had turned. From there, I travelled by instinct because we had only the sketch. Road signs were rare.

"You can't trust signs anyway, Sister. Sometimes they're turned to mislead you," Henri said.

Our radiator overheated. No problem. We pulled over to let it cool.

"Henri, please get the jug of water we put in the back. It's close to the door."

Henri returned to show me the empty jug. Its bung had worked loose, and the jug had fallen over.

"We'll let the radiator cool more and then proceed slowly until we find water. If we're a little late, it won't matter," I said.

I pictured Ernst and Jones detouring to an army roadhouse or secret restaurant. We would feast on a tin of rations.

I noticed the furrow in Henri's brow as we drove like a wounded animal. "This is Allies' territory now, so we're safe." My voice wavered.

Henri pointed to a stone cottage. "Sister Della, we could ask there for water. Most French are on our side."

The agèd woman who answered the door opened her arms, her larder, her heart when she saw my uniform. Of course we could have water, but only if we also shared her *potage* which bubbled on her stove.

How could we have refused her invitation and the scent of her soup?

Henri topped up our radiator while I visited with Madame. She stretched the soup with water, potatoes, and a variety of dried herbs.

"This is delicious, Madame. What goes in it?"

"Mostly potatoes, but I like to gather herbs and wild greens still found on the muddy land. My soup's never the same. Don't be shy. You must have bread, too."

With our thank you, we gave her several tins of rations and meat. I felt as safe as I'd ever be in France. And humbled, as well as thankful.

**Marie Mossman**

We parked our truck in front of the church for our rendezvous with Dr. Ernst. "Henri, I bet you five French francs our doctors will arrive *after* a half hour. If they arrive before, I'll pay you five, O.K.?"

While we waited, I asked him to tell me about his son.

# 41: Timing ourselves

"I spoiled my boy after his mother died," Henri told me. "He was used to getting his own way, you see. He wanted to sign up when posters were everywhere, and his friends wore natty army uniforms. At first I said. 'It's not for you. War's ugly.' I had a cousin killed in Africa, and men from our village went in glory to Indochina. Most were killed and rotted there. But he insisted over and over, so I finally gave in. I told him, 'It'll break my heart if you're hurt.' My heart was broken a month after he enlisted."

"But you volunteered for war service, Henri."

"To help the wounded. I've no fondness for war. I'd rather be killed than damage another man. My helping you and the doctors is a poultice on my pain."

"You must see a glimmer of hope."

"Only in rumours of armistice. If it happens, you'll see me smile and dance, and enjoy eating again, Sister Della."

"I'll dance a jig with you, too, when armistice is announced. It's a promise."

Then we sat quiet for several minutes, until I shook him awake to ask, "Do you hear a motor?"

Ernst stopped the ambulance beside us on the twenty-ninth minute of my bet.

"Follow us!" His tone was harried.

He led us west of town to a spot more open than our other sites had been. There was little choice if the brass wanted us in this area, because the flat fields surrounding us were muddy, pock-marked, and stripped of greenery, fatigued from five years of war, like the local population.

"We'll erect the tent ourselves, play Boy Scouts. Our work crew's busy entertaining Huns. Ask me later."

Ernst demonstrated a sharp eye for right angles and support depths while he supervised Henri and Jones. We all helped position the canvas. I hung material from the ceiling and wooden supports with twine, to separate my accommodation for the night.

"We may operate from the ambulance tomorrow, but there's a chance the chaps'll show up with our other tents and gear by morning."

I set our midget gas cooker in the corner, close to the door flap. We warmed our rations on this mighty device.

I looked at the familiar unattractive mess in my tin. *We're lucky to have food. We're lucky to have food. We're lucky...*

Ernst caught my eye. "I'll tell you two about our mis-adventure this afternoon, lest you think we were leisurely consuming gourmet French cuisine, if that were possible these days."

I smiled.

"First, though, there's one important matter. This is the fifth time the Allied Forces have fought the Germans in Flanders. The Huns are desperate for a win, so they might resort to poison gas as they've done before. For God's sake, if you smell anything strange tonight, alert the rest of us. Don't be prissy. Pee on your handkerchief and tie it around your face. Urine neutralizes chlorine."

"Why not use a mask?"

"Yes, but we need a refresher drill to put 'em on properly. We'll have one first thing in the morning."

He turned to Henri. "You may retire."

"Sister?" Ernst held up his whisky bottle.

"Thanks, I'll make tea."

"You may not believe this. We stopped at an *estaminet*. From the outside, we heard yelling and singing. Trouble was, it might've been Scottish or Flemish, as far as we could tell. Another thing, a white rag hung on the front door. We peeked through a window before entering. Wise decision. The place was polluted with a half dozen German soldiers, plastered! The largest fellow stood, singing, with a beer stein in his hand.

"Jones opened the door, yelled 'Hands up!' and I shot the giant's stein out of his mitt. Curiously, one of the Germans also shouted, 'Hands up!' Twelve hands went up: five pairs, and one single hand that belonged to the corporal. His other one was tied to the back of his chair. The corporal's torso and bare feet were secured to his chair with his puttees. He didn't look happy, though with his free hand he reached for beer, cheese, and bread placed on the bench before him."

"Was there another hand somewhere?"

"Always so precise, Sister. Might have known you'd do the math. I'll get to the other hand in a minute."

"Didn't they have guns?"

"A pile of trench knives, Mauser rifles, ammo and one pistol in the corner farthest away from their corporal. These guys were surrendering, on full bellies, I might add."

"The host hadn't resisted them?"

"Germans have invaded the locals, and the Allies have freed, them several times. Locals submit to whoever comes with guns. The host said these Germans burst in, guns blazing, but later realized they were abandoned in Allied territory. The men, youngsters really, saw more food there than they'd been used to, so decided to tie up their corporal and surrender. Our arrival produced the script they'd written for their play."

"Is that what the host really said?"

"In general, yes. He said they apologized when they tied his feet to the bar and secured one arm behind his back. His was the twelfth hand raised, after Jones's order, Sister. He was free to hand over liquor and glasses and tell the boys where to find food."

"What have you done with the Germans?"

"I'd arranged to meet our supply truck crew at that *estaminet*, so we tied the boys tighter than they'd secured their corporal, and we waited for our crew. Our men'll find a place for the Huns, though nobody wants to babysit prisoners these days."

He poured another whisky for himself and Jones, who'd been smiling at Ernst's recap. "Our gear should be set up by noon tomorrow. We'll operate before the afternoon's out. Won't be any shortage of bodies to work on."

"I'll dig out my masks and turn in," I said.

"We want to hear you having a good pee in the right place, Sister."

"I return the concern, sir."

I grabbed my gas masks next morning. My regular model, the latest American Small Box respirator, filtered air through processed peach stones. I required a medium-size mask. My reserve one was the French M2.

"Team," Dr. Ernst said, "the brass have ordered this retraining. You're to have your masks within grabbing distance at all times and are expected to put one on in six seconds. Any longer and you risk chemical burning of your eyes, skin, lungs. Death even. Jones, demonstrate the alert position."

Jones hung his American apparatus from his neck.

"Correct. If any of us detect gas we're to alert the others. Practice time."

Ernst grabbed a metal container, banged it and yelled. "Gas attack!"

I knew what to do, but my hands fumbled. Six seconds flashed by. My mask was far from tightly secured.

We took turns warning, and timing ourselves, until everyone's fingers remembered the motions perfectly.

"You're ready for testing with gas."

I remembered previous training with chemicals that smelled horrible and actually burned and I wondered what Ernst would use.

"We're using camphor. Chlorine would be more realistic, but I want you in shape for surgery this afternoon."

Ernst called the warning, then went around with his bottle of camphor. No one passed the test the first time, but by noon, everyone got the mask on properly, within six seconds.

"Just in time. Jones, Sister, Henri, let's have lunch. I expect the chaps in the truck we see coming will want a break before they set up our tents."

The gas training had tensed my nerves, but I knew focusing on work would suppress my fears. I reminded myself to treat each patient as I would Charlie or Cousin Geoffrey.

Munitions exploded in the distance.

# 42: Any suggestions?

Days disappeared, consumed by eighteen hours of surgery: amputations, wound cleansing, and, most satisfying of all, reconstruction of long bones. Our cases included German casualties abandoned by their retreating troops. Ernst operated on all wounded with equal care and saved limbs most surgeons would have amputated.

I felt integral to the surgical team, though I took tea instead of the whisky Ernst and Jones preferred each night, and I never could be part of the doctors' reminiscences.

I enjoyed Ernst's jokes, even the acerbic or risqué ones. How did we remain respectful in all important ways in such intimate circumstances? I became fond of Dr. Ernst, his calmness, dedication, and priceless skills.

We were finishing surgery one day when Henri announced. "Dr. Ernst, two men have driven up. I think one is your commander."

The official, with a grave expression, handed a letter to Ernst, who read it. The doctor offered refreshment to his commander, who refused.

"Then I thank you, sir, for you kindness. And now, if you will excuse me, I must return to surgery." Every facial muscle was tense.

He worked as precisely as ever, but in slow motion. When the technical part was completed, he did something I'd never before seen him do. He patted the soldier on his shoulder. "There, son, you'll have your leg. Good luck."

"Excuse me." He went into his room in the tent to re-read his letter.

After a few minutes, I heard bangs and thuds as if items were being hurled, then the yell. "Jones, come have a drink!"

I tidied the surgery and, with Henri, cared for patients and triaged new casualty arrivals. I felt vulnerable that night, with Ernst in no state to protect me, and wished for the Browning Charlie had offered.

I decided to knee Jones in the genitals if he bothered me; however, the doctors depleted their supply of whisky, and then slept, so I was safe.

Ernst explained in the morning, "My wife's dead. Spanish influenza. She felt unwell one day, was dead the next."

I reached out to touch his shoulder. He bent down, put his arms around me and wailed like a grief-stricken lion. Henri and Jones kept a distance.

I let Ernst hold on to me for comfort. Whose?

"She was beautiful...glossy long blond hair. Was used to money, parties, saw life on the cheery side. Insisted on having a maid and cook.

Said, 'Act like a workhorse and they'll treat you like a workhorse.' She's gone."

I thought I'd learned to protect myself from another's grief, but his stripped my defences. I shared his raw pain.

He wept again.

"Remember, you have two sons."

"But *she's* gone!"

"Let it out." What else could one say?

We were performing lifesaving surgery by noon. Ernst worked slowly, deliberately, as though he were forcing himself to focus. There was no light talk, no joking. His shoulders slumped and he walked mechanically. I sensed he could not continue at the CCS after the loss of his wife.

We heard an armistice was being negotiated. Our spirits soared.

"It was only a rumour," a messenger informed us. Our spirits dived.

Ernst exhibited the joy of a Dickensian workhouse. He conversed like a polite automaton and emanated the darkness of a nighttime medieval village. I strove for equilibrium. Jones revealed a sympathetic side.

"What'll you do, Della, when the war ends?"

I didn't answer immediately, as I was counting supplies.

"Do you have plans for after armistice?" he continued. "I don't mean to be nosy, but maybe Ernst or I could help you."

"I haven't thought much about it. Any suggestions?"

"Ernst and I go back to our practices, but you have to find a job. If you're stuck, look us up. We could put in a good word for you at our hospital. I think you're the best. I mean it: the best as a surgical nurse, and as a person."

"Thank you, Dr. Jones. I *have* heard rumours the government'll demobilize rapidly and nurses'll be dismissed. They'll want to reduce costs."

"Ernst and I have written for passage on the first boat home."

"I'll stay in France as long as the Red Cross needs me here for nursing. There'll be additional work to clarify where soldiers fell. Families want that information confirmed."

An official messenger told us all hostilities would stop at eleven hundred hours on November 11, 1918. The relief, the joy!

But soldiers arrived with casualties up to the last minute, and after. "People are already celebrating in Ypres," a messenger said, "and there'll be an official celebration tomorrow! Come in for it."

I prepared to care for our patients on November 12, and then lit my tiny oil lamp to write to the Matron in Chief in London. Would she grant my request to remain in France as long as nurses were needed?

~

"I don't feel like celebrating," Ernst said, "and Jones'll stay with me. You and Henri go in and enjoy yourselves."

I would have happily walked the few miles, but Ernst commanded us to take the truck, so Henri and I stocked it with rations just to be sure, and headed over the border to Belgium for the most joyous party of my life.

**Marie Mossman**

# 43: To dance

A mixture of human voices and musical instruments greeted us as we approached the bombed city. In addition to English and French, songs broke out in Flemish.

Dancing sprung up in the public square all day: step dancing, circle dancing, couple dancing. The dances reminded me of parties at home when people of all ages danced with each other.

"I wonder what that one's called," I mused.

Henri shrugged.

A stranger told me, "It's the Seven Leaps, a traditional dance. Might be Dutch originally. We're a young country, so we borrow traditions from other places, like you in America."

"I'm here with the Americans, but I'm Canadian."

"Canada helped us in the war a lot. Stay for the day. There'll be speeches and wonderful music later. Look over there: the children are dancing the Pink Hat."

A Belgian army band played and thousands sang "*La Brabançonne*", Belgium's national anthem. I remember how proud the people stood; how their clear voices filled the air with joyful emotion. And then, the crowd hushed when a Belgian official climbed onto the flatbed of a truck and stood still. He wore a khaki uniform distinguished by shoulder tabs with shiny buttons.

I remember a gist of his speech that day, given in a firm voice:

*Fellow citizens and honourable guests, today, we live the greatest joy imaginable and express eternal gratitude to those who have freed us from the Kaiser's threat. Brave citizens returned to live in Ypres this past year. The huts they occupy have been built through money in our reconstruction fund. The huts will be replaced in time with properly constructed homes.*

He concluded with an even stronger tone. "I promise you, my friends, we will rebuild."

I tensed when shouting broke out behind us. Three thin youths, dressed in ill-fitting clothing, had ventured into town to beg food. People figured out the lads were German soldiers and began to harass them.

The officer raised his hand for quiet. "Hostilities have ended and we must work together for peace. Guards, provide these men with bread and water, then escort them to the road leading to their homeland. We are Belgians. We will treat all people with respect. Now, let's enjoy our celebration."

Henri grabbed my hand to dance. Violins and accordions again produced music in all directions. We jigged around to twenty rhythms at once. Who needed to know the steps?

A stranger grabbed me and I twirled with him. Henri bobbed in the distance, stomping and hopping with men, women, or children. The music gave us energy to move as we hadn't imagined we could. Eventually, we step-danced our way back together.

I sniffed a sweet scent drifting by. "We must try them," Henri said.

Entrepreneurs were hawking a sugar- dusted sweet they called waffle. Bakers cooked them on braziers set up in crannies around the town square.

Henri came back with a waffle for each of us. He refused my money. "I bought them with the five francs I won from you." And smiled as though he'd bested me again.

We headed for our truck at sixteen hundred hours, as darkness enveloped. "What's keeping you so quiet, Henri?"

"I'm thinking about what my life will be like. No wife, no son, just my farm, and maybe there won't even be a house. What'll you do, Sister?"

"Nursing of some sort. There'll be a need, but I understand governments and armies will lay off nurses as fast as they can, to save money. I've applied to stay on in France. You must decide soon what you want to do next."

"Yes, Sister."

We drove on in a silence that was grasping for future plans.

# 44: New beginning

We expected orders shortly after Armistice was confirmed, so were relieved when they arrived on November 22. Ernst read. "You are to effect deconstruction of your CCS and to report with staff and salvageable equipment to #12 General Hospital. You and your team members, will individually receive reassignment orders at the Hospital."

The brass did not specify whether the United States or England was responsible for me.

Ernst said, "I hate the bureaucracy in these damned enormous hospitals!" He buried himself in paperwork.

"Shall I pack your equipment and meds as well as Ernst's?" I asked Jones.

"Sure, Sister. I trust you."

He and Henri focused on preparing patients for transport. We were packed for Rouen when army crews arrived to dismantle tents and take other gear for transportation.

Ernst briefed us the night before departure. "We're driving southwest and will avoid larger towns. We anticipate four to eight hours driving and will leave at daybreak to ensure we get to Rouen before dark. Gas up at every opportunity and use your reserve petrol only if necessary. Sister, Henri will ride with you."

I asked if we would go in convoy.

"Yes, but if we're separated, head straight to #12 General."

Henri scraped frost off our windscreen the next morning. I put the truck into gear and was ready to charge forward when Ernst hopped out of his ambulance.

"You're not to pick up any travellers. Got it?"

"Sir." I nodded.

"Is the jug of radiator water properly secured?" I asked Henri.

"Yes, Sister, and I put an extra one here." He pointed between his feet.

Ernst sped off in the ambulance like the last time we convoyed. I couldn't keep up with him.

"We'll be okay," I told myself. We had canned rations in our vehicle, and any local person could direct us to Rouen.

As our truck rumbled along, Henri was silent, so I kept my eyes on the pock-marked and muddy countryside, abnormal, but war-torn normal. Grass and trees were dressed in brown and golden colours, greyed by heavy mist.

My toes and fingertips became numb from cold. I wondered whether I could I endure another winter in Europe, and hoped for heat wherever I would stay.

"Henri, I've an idea. Want to hear it?"

"Yes."

"When you go home, the nuns'll be taking care of war veterans, won't they?"

"I think, yes, Sister."

"You've learned a lot about care of sick men. If you find life on your farm too quiet, you could help the nuns. What do you think?"

"Maybe."

We were past St. Omer when I spotted an ambulance on the side of the road with its radiator steaming like a locomotive.

Ernst waved us down. His voice was brusque. "You'll have to take me to the nearest place where I can get water."

Henri whispered. "May I?"

I nodded.

The old fellow kept a solemn face as he raised our spare water jug. "Doctor Ernst, can you use this? We have another."

"Why, thank you, Henri."

Ernst turned to me. "Sister, we'll be back on the road in a minute. Follow us. I sense a restaurant coming up."

We stopped in Hesdin. A Canadian crew was in town to repair the railway and they occupied all the eating places.

"We're improving the line into Etaples," one of the crew told us. "There's a lot of work to do. In the last months the Germans planted mines on the tracks."

"Is it far to Etaples?" I asked.

"Maybe fifteen miles that way, on the coast." He pointed.

My heart took a leap. How could I find out if Charlie were there, without triggering questions?

"Henri, I've heard so much about Etaples. Since we'll be close by, maybe we'll get a chance to visit it sometime."

"Never know the future."

We drove on through a countryside that displayed as many burnt-out villages and dugouts as it did the bucolic farms seen on postcards. We found a table at the restaurant Mado in Abbeville.

Dr. Ernst insisted the four of us dine together, and declared. "It's on Jones and me, we've agreed."

Jones' jaw dropped, but he concurred, after a moment.

When the waiter approached, Ernst ordered soup for four, then told Henri. "You know the food here better than we do. Choose the rest."

Henri asked Ernst if he liked fish, then ordered. "For the doctor, sole with potatoes and a glass of a white wine." He added, "The fish should be fresh in this area."

"I'll have the same," Jones said.

Henri looked to me. "The fish? Or maybe the stew?"

Our waiter spoke up. "Our cook starts a stew every morning. It won't take long."

I nodded. "Stew's warming and has vegetables. I'll have it and herbal tea, if possible."

Henri relayed. "A stew, and herbal tea for Madame." Then he added. "For myself, another bowl of soup. It tastes homemade." He put his fingertips to his lips and smacked. "And, if it's not rationed, lots of your good bread."

We three others agreed to give Henri our bread rations as well. I sent a silent blessing skyward, then thanked Dr. Ernst and Dr. Jones for providing lunch.

Ernst raised his wineglass. "To our new beginning."

"Wonder what the brass have planned," I said.

We agreed #12 would be a short-lived assignment for Ernst and Jones, and my duties might change as demobilization progressed.

Henri spoke up. "When they discharge me, I'll go back to my farm. Some of my family may still live in the area, or I might find a widow who'd welcome an old man." The corners of his mouth curved upward, and his eyes gleamed.

"Or the nuns might need help," I said, straight-faced.

He shrugged his shoulders and looked at me.

I became quiet, lost in the pleasure of good food among supportive colleagues. Three of us finished with apple pie and coffee while Henri sipped a local eau de vie.

Ernst stood up. "It'd be nice to linger, but the sun'll set in a few hours. We've a distance to go to Rouen, and must find our hospital among dozens."

"Excuse me, sir," said the waiter when Ernst was paying. "I understand you're a doctor. The Australian hospital here is overcrowded with Spanish influenza cases. Could you possibly stop to help out?"

"I'm sorry, lad, we've orders to continue to Rouen and should get there before dark today. We really must carry on. Thank you for such a wonderful meal. I wish you well."

"Dr. Ernst sent a lot of men to Etaples from our parades," Henri said when we were seated in our truck.

"Yes, he did. We'll go there if we get the opportunity." I lurched the truck forward on the last leg to Rouen, and new adventures.

# 45: No promises

I felt reckless, but had managed to keep within view of Ernst's vehicle since Abbeville.

Driving the Ford required me to use my eyes, two hands, and feet, avoid injury, control speed, and ensure the machine was maintained. I'd learned all these skills earlier—on the farm, sewing on Katherine's Singer, or using medical devices. I wondered whether driving would be thought an ordinary skill if more women had money to buy a car and learn to drive.

Ernst stopped abruptly at a paint -starved village café, and I pulled up beside him.

"Your driving has improved tremendously, Sister."

"It felt more like a convoy today."

"This burg is on the outskirts of Rouen, so we'll have soup here, save #12 the trouble of heating up rations."

"Thoughtful of you, Dr. Ernst."

"Do what I can to save army food for those who have no choice. Let's get inside."

The bar was a prominent part of the café's one public room. We sat at a small, dark, wood table, and Ernst ordered four bowls of soup. "Make sure it's really hot."

"Our chef sources excellent potatoes locally, and uses herbs to make exceptional soup, sir. It's kept just below the boil to develop a rich fla-vour. I guarantee you'll be pleased with our soup."

Light and hot, it suited me fine after my heavy lunch.

I was sad to think ahead to the end of our team, because we'd worked closely and well together. What would I do now, with the war over? The question churned in my subconscious, and invaded my conscious brain. The uncertainty of peacetime produced more anxiety than I'd anticip-ated.

"We may as well forge on and see what Matron has in store for us," Ernst said.

We rose and headed for our vehicles.

The countryside changed little until we saw a narrow, low shed, then a field of sheds, then fields of sheds—the hospitals of Rouen.

~

Matron invited us to meet with her as soon as we'd arranged for a work crew to store our supplies. "Henri," she said, "we thank you for your volunteer work during our struggle against the Germans. You're welcome to continue here for a week, and then we must ask you to leave because our orderlies are usually VD patients, and we have plenty. They're easily identified by their distinctive tie. We can provide you with a small compensation from our funds and free passage to your place of enlisting. There's also the possibility of a Medal of Gratitude. We're truly grateful for your volunteer work. You may now go to the front desk and ask for someone to show you accommodation."

My spine and lips became rigid when I heard her dismiss him so briefly. He had given all he could, and had lost his son. He was a hero.

"I'll miss you, Henri. You've been my helper and my security during the madness. God bless you," I said.

Matron smiled in a kindly manner and added. "Good luck, Henri."

She turned her attention to us who remained. "I'd like to have a duplicate of each of you because we've lost so many doctors and nurses to the Spanish influenza, and your excellent reputations have preceded you. However, you'll no longer work consistently as a team."

She consulted her notes. "Dr. Jones, I've received your orders. You'll remain at #12 General until the morning of 8 December, and you'll be scheduled to assist with surgeries. Check the roster after breakfast tomorrow. On the 8th, you'll be issued a voucher for travel to Brest where you'll board, as ship's doctor, the USS *Walter D. Munson*, which is expected to depart shortly afterwards. You'll be in New York by Christmas. I'm delighted to have your assistance for the short time you remain here. You may go now to the front desk and ask directions to your room."

"Is the *Munson* a—?"

"I gather it's a small cargo vessel. I am delighted you're able to go home, but regret you can't be assigned the luxury of an ocean liner."

Jones pulled down the corners of his mouth and slumped his shoulders, but I spotted a twinkle in his eyes. He wasn't one to seek the silver service. "Dr. Ernst, we await word on the status of your leave request. In the meantime, you'll be scheduled for our most challenging surgical cases, and that will include repairing work done by unskilled medics under pressure to save a man's life. I'm grateful to have a surgeon of your skill on staff. For now, you, too, are directed to the front desk for a room assignment. Check the surgery roster after breakfast. Good night."

I decided I'd take whatever she gave me so I could investigate where Charlie was or what had happened to him. I could send money to help out at home, and put a little aside for the future, if I stayed on. One never knew...

*I can't go back to life in East Cove. Always did want more action. I might visit home in summer, though. I can handle the Deacon if he tries anything.*

"Sister Della, you wish to prolong your assignment in France. We can use you here as long as the Spanish influenza rages, but I make no promises for long-term employment. We're demobilizing, you understand."

I nodded.

"I see you're highly recommended as a surgical assistant, and are an experienced night supervisor and a meticulous organizer of medical supplies and writer of notes. Your exceptional academic achievements may lead to work in records research when demand for your more practical nursing skills becomes less urgent. At this hospital, you're assigned duty as night supervisor. However, if you're called to assist at surgery, give that priority. A replacement supervisor will be called in. Off you go now, and find yourself a room."

"Thank you, Matron."

I had an unsettling dream that night. A pregnant woman in difficult labour arrived at #12 General. She delivered a baby, probably a girl. The infant suffered extreme stress during birth and a shoulder—I wasn't sure which one—would likely wither. The girl had an oval birthmark on her right wrist, like the one I'd noticed on Charlie at Stonehenge. When someone in the dream asked who the father was, the new mother said, 'Charles Rafuse.' The mother died and the orphan survived.

*It's only a nightmare. Don't pay attention.*

I couldn't erase the memory of the dream. My mind kept searching for meaning and speculating what I'd do if the dream contained truth. Was it within me to accept the child as my ward? And would it be possible, as she would have grandparents, assuming her father was the Charles Rafuse I knew? Could I find care for her while I was working in the States, and take her home with me during my vacations?

I warmed to the idea of young company when I wasn't working. Gossips at home would spread nasty rumours, but most people would accept the arrangement if I explained.

This was all so unlikely, I willed the whole affair to a back corner of my mind.

I looked around #12 General the next morning. My accommodation was an improvement on the CCS tent room. Here, my cubical was a few square feet larger.

The hospital consisted of numerous one-storied wooden sheds with metal roofs. We had a mess building and stoves for heat. Still, I slept in my uniform for warmth.

I was scheduled to assist at surgery the next afternoon, and then to supervise in a recovery ward that night. Matron explained. "We who are healthy do double shifts. We're short of nurses."

I thought it curious, but army-like. They were sending nurses back to the United States at the same time they were short staffed in France.

I fitted into routines so readily that memories of my early difficulties at Fargo seemed preposterous. Why had the English resented me in their hospital? Why had I, a British subject, found their language so difficult?

From the distance of time, I saw learning and stretching of minds on both sides. Having my mind broadened wasn't a benefit of war I'd anticipated. I would no longer so quickly judge others negatively: the person who committed suicide; the girl who "got into trouble"; a man who stole food because he was hungry, or to feed a child; couples who indulged in sex before the preacher approved.

I still found mercy killings and killing in self-defence abominable, but I no longer recognized absolute truths.

I nursed every day or night, a "normal" workload; even so, it was less demanding than my days on our CCS team. Winter in France continued raw and cold and I treasured hot tea or cocoa on breaks, as much for the pleasure of warming my hands as for the flavour. I enjoyed scheduled night supervision shifts, with added sudden requests to assist surgery.

Ernst operated on wounds that had been closed during surgeries in CCSs, but were festering. He routinely ordered the limb x-rayed, then operated to remove debris if metal was recorded on the radiograph. I regarded these debris operations as unchallenging for Ernst or me, much like life in general after Armistice.

"Sister Della, Matron says you're to assist at surgery."

This nerve repair operation energized me, and revealed an aspect of Ernst's personality I hadn't observed before. We rushed to a private who had sustained a cut below the elbow of his dominant arm. Ernst was scrubbing up and I scrubbed, too, at emergency speed.

Blood flow under control, I set up the Dakin's drip. Ernst cleaned the wound. It was fresher and less dirty than those from the trenches. He examined the wound visually, and confirmed reduced function by asking the patient to move his fingers and to identify warmth and cold by touch.

Ernst diagnosed a severed median nerve. "The cut ends are unlikely to spontaneously reunite, but we must give Nature its best chance."

Our anaesthetist administered sedation. I laid out sterile instruments and silk thread for suturing.

Ernst gently positioned the nerve ends together, supported them, and closed the arm wound, using the fine silk thread. We protected the arm with a splint, then the patient was removed to post-operation observation.

Throughout the operation, Ernst was more gentle than I'd ever observed. "I've been wanting to do this procedure. The nerves *may* rejoin." He shrugged, did not smile. "We have a lot to learn about nerve treatment."

He took paper and a pen. "I'll write instructions for his care here, and request therapy, so he's more likely to get it when he arrives home. Excellent back up, Sister Della. You may return to your ward now or take a break, if rules allow."

"Sir." I nodded.

He cleared his throat. "We should have a chat, Sister. Maybe a quiet dinner, good food."

"Sounds tempting, Dr. Ernst. I'd need time to arrange leave."

"Understood."

I returned to my ward with Ernst's suggestion tucked away in a back corner of my brain. My immediate concern was to complete documentation for patients scheduled for discharge, for their transportation home.

Ernst loped toward me on a wooden walkway several days after the nerve operation. I noted fatigue in his face. "Hi, Del. How's my best surgery assistant? Don't tell anyone I said that. We're not supposed to have favourites."

"Fine, Ernst, and yourself?"

"I have a bad case of restaurant withdrawal symptoms. I need you to come to town with me for some real food."

"There's the matter of the leave, sir."

"We haven't had much of a break since we arrived at #12. Let's request time off early New Year's Eve. We don't want to be out late like the youngsters. I speak for myself on that last bit."

"If you're serious, sir, I'll ask. You're skilled at choosing superior eating places."

"Of course I'm serious! Send me a note when you have approval. Must go."

I'd never before had plans for New Year's Eve. People said the party in Rouen after Armistice had been wild. I wondered what New Year's Eve would be like.

# 46: Verbal joust

"I'm glad you're able to join me this evening, Della. The brass may order me out immediately when my leave's granted. We mightn't have a chance to say goodbye."

"We'll have a pleasant evening, I'm sure, Ernst."

The waiter stepped over to our table and Ernst ordered. "We'll start with soup, then oysters for myself, and foie gras for Madame. And for the main course, quail with lentils for both of us, and a bottle of good local red wine. For dessert we'll have ice cream with preserved fruit, and a liqueur."

"We've been through a lot together, Del," he said. "Experiences no one else might understand."

"True. frozen in time." I rubbed my hands together.

"You're an excellent surgical nurse. Never forget it."

"Thank you, Ernst. I admire your skill, and devotion to caring work."

"Della, you could have stayed in the States, said work here would be too strenuous. Or that you didn't think it was America's war. Many people made excuses in the beginning. Tell me, why did you come over?"

"There wasn't any one reason. The pressure from propaganda was tremendous, as you know. Young men from Nova Scotia enlisted, even my cousin Geoffrey. When I saw him last, he was maybe thirteen years old. He was wounded in '15. Canada's part of the British Empire, and lots of people at home were born in England. Their war was our war. I felt it, though I'd been living in the States for ten years by then."

"I think there's more."

"Maybe I was pulled by the promise of adventure, the allure of doing something that really counted. I signed up as soon as I could, when the age limit for nurses was raised. Possibly the beautiful uniform attracted me. Silly."

"Were you escaping anything?"

"Boredom, perhaps. That's the other side of seeking adventure, isn't it?"

"Could be, unless there was something truly unpleasant in your life."

The Deacon flashed through my mind. "No, nothing that sent me over here."

"Okay, we'll leave it. Are you warmed by the soup?"

"Yes! It was what I needed. The French make a simple soup special every time. We'll have to go slowly with this feasting tonight, won't we?"

We sat in friendly silence a minute or so, until I ventured, "Ernst, what were your reasons?"

"As you say, there was the pressure of propaganda and the allure of doing surgery that really counted. I knew I'd want proper care for my sons if they were here."

"Anything else?"

"Maybe I wanted to impress my wife and her family. Not that it matters now."

"I shouldn't have—"

"Not at all. Here come our oysters and foie gras. I'll have a white wine with my oysters. Would you like something to drink?"

"A glass of water would be nice, thanks. The foie gras looks rich."

"Sometimes correspondence came addressed to Della R. Schwester. What did the R. stand for?"

"Rosemarie. I don't know where the name comes from, though there were a couple of great-great aunts called Maria. Why do you ask?"

"The R stood out. My wife's name was Rose."

"And the C on your messages?"

"For Charles, my first name. Once people know me, they usually call me Ernst and ignore the Charles part."

"Charles!"

"Yes. Why? Was it your father's name?"

"No, no. But I've met a couple other important people called Charles. It's more than a coincidence."

"You're too sensible to believe in any sort of nonsense. It's a common name. I'm ready for quail, aren't you?"

"The waiter's coming with a tray right now."

The waiter placed our plates on the white linen tablecloth. Saliva poured into my mouth. The waiter offered the red wine to Ernst for approval, filled our glasses, wished us bon appétit, and backed away.

We had arrived when the restaurant was empty of patrons; by this time, all the tables were occupied. A few people were eating their first course. Others waited to have their orders taken.

"I've become fond of you, Del, in a brotherly sort of way. If you ever have a serious problem, if anyone gives you a hard time, you must let me know. I'll help you out."

"Kind of you, Ernst."

"You don't spend money on yourself, but you send it back to Canada. You must have people there you care about."

"I come from a large family and we keep in touch."

"Good to know. I won't probe further, but remember what I said about helping you if you need support, won't you?"

"Thank you, I will, Ernst."

"I mean it, Del. We medical people are always observing. I've a feeling something deep troubles you. Maybe it's not the reason why you served in the war, perhaps someone threatened you early on."

"You're a psychiatrist as well as a surgeon! I didn't know you were watching me so much." I chuckled and smiled at him.

Quail. I never had it before or afterwards, because of the expense. It looked like a plump miniature adult chicken, roasted to perfection, golden brown, glistening from a sweet-salty glaze.

"You present in a guarded manner, self-controlled, wear a cool mask. I ask. 'Where's the real Del?' You show your skill, efficiency, a caring manner, your intelligence even, in a verbal joust, but what's Del like at the core? Why haven't I seen the unprotected Della? Maybe you don't like men?"

"Maybe there's only what you see."

I was about to try a slice of the breast meat when Ernst's voice, in a softened tone, reached my astonished ears. "I'm fond of you, Del, but my feelings, I confess, are far from brotherly. Truth is, I'm strongly attracted to you."

*You're a powerful magnet yourself, but I'm not about to tell you!*

I straightened my spine. "We've been through a lot together."

"Exactly. I've seen you under the most gruelling situations that might bring out the worst in a person, and all I've seen is someone whose company I need."

"You're embarrassing me now, Ernst."

"No need. Del, I've fallen in love with you. Can I top up your glass?"

"Not now, thanks. I'm not used to much alcohol."

Ernst reached over and placed his hand on my right one, that held my knife. "Don't pretend you don't know what this means, Del. I think of you whenever there's a break in work and sometimes in the middle of surgery. You're invading my brain like you've invaded my heart. We have to do something about this, this strong attraction."

"Let's enjoy New Year's Eve without making things complicated. Things'll seem different in the morning."

"Complicated. You told me once your life was complicated, but never explained. Is it less complicated now? Whether it is or not, does it matter?"

"There *is* still a complication." My heart, stomach, and gut tensed.

Our waiter rescued me by walking over with our ice cream and the restaurant's special compôte of fruit preserved in brandy! I'd never had brandied fruit before. Our homemade ice cream in Nova Scotia, with fresh strawberries was every bit as delicious, but who wanted to judge?

Ernst reminded our waiter about the liqueur.

"I'll pass on liqueur, because of my night duty," I said.

Ernst removed a notebook from his breast pocket and wrote. "Here's my hospital in Philly. It's likely I'll move to California, but they'd forward a letter. I've written, also, the names of my sons, so you have another way to contact me if you want to get in touch."

"Thank you, Ernst. Would you like my family's address in Nova Scotia? The town's all you need, 'cause everyone knows us, and the postmistress is our neighbour. You might vacation there sometime. It's wonderful in July and August."

He wrote East Bay in his notebook.

"You have coffee or tea while I enjoy a Calvados. Then we can wander over to the early movie at the Omnia. You'll be back to #12 in time for duty, wide awake from caffeine."

"Some of the women in my residence loved *Good Night, Nurse!* with Buster Keaton. They said it gave them a good laugh."

"The Keaton movie's finished, and no one could tell me what the new film is. We'll find out soon enough."

We sipped our drinks and then strolled to the Omnia at dusk. Ernst put his hand on my shoulder, but attempted no other liberties.

On the way, a Rouennais fell into step with us. "Going to L'Omnia?" he asked. He was thin, but muscular, dressed in workman's overalls covered with stone dust. "The theatre was bombed in August, but they fixed it up quickly. I like the new stained glass better than the nude dancer that was there before. You'll see."

He resumed his faster pace.

The cinema was a stunning, three-storey stone building. One corner of it, a domed tower, reached upward yet another storey, as if it were com-peting with cinemas of Paris or New York.

"Let's have a look at the new window," I said. It depicted Jeanne d'Arc, Pierre Corneille, and a modern French soldier sailing together in a classic Normand-style boat called a *drakkar*.

"I might've preferred the nude female dancer," Ernst said.

"I might, too, if there were a nude male with her."

"Oh, starting one of your verbal jousts, are you?"

"Fair's fair."

Ernst went ahead to buy tickets. I looked at a poster for the new movie, *The Firefly of France*, and deduced it would be a tense drama. It was from Paramount Pictures. I wondered whether the theatre had a pianist.

We chose centre seats about halfway back. No one sat next to us, to my relief, as Spanish influenza continued to rage in Rouen. I welcomed the excuse to focus on something other than conversation with Ernst.

During a calm moment in the movie, however, I turned to look at him. His head rested on the back of his seat and his mouth was open. The pianist was playing softly, when Ernst produced a high volume, vibrating snore. The pianist increased volume, but not before dozens of heads had swivelled in our direction.

"Did you poke me?"

"Only to save your good reputation, sir."

The movie ended shortly after secret papers were delivered to the correct French authorities; however, Ernst's project continued. "I've reserved a space where we can enjoy a quiet hour together to end our special night."

"Tell me more." I tried a smile, but inwardly tensed.

"I've booked a room at the *Hôtel aux Papillons*, where I'll have my nightcap and order whatever you like. It'll be private and a nice end to the evening."

"That shows foresight, Ernst, but I prefer to return directly to the hospital." My shoulders were squared.

"We may not have an opportunity again. My leave to America should come through any day. We could provide comfort to each other. What would be wrong with that?"

"I've thought such things through and have decided not to judge others, but for me certain intimacies occur only within a long-term commitment."

"Del, my dear, I already know you better than I ever did my wife, as much as I loved her. We've a chance to create a wonderful memory this evening. If the war has taught me anything, it's how life may be cut short. We must enjoy it while we're here."

"If we're meant to have a more intimate connection, another opportunity will present itself. You're a magnetic person, Ernst. I'm sure many attractive ladies walking the streets this evening would be happy to accommodate you."

"You're a hard woman, Del."

My voice softened. "Why don't we go to a café for your whisky? I'll have tea and then return to #12."

Ernst gave up his Don Juan attempt. I compromised on one last conflict that occurred after he had his drink.

"You've taught me so well, Ernst, I'd like to drive back."

"No, no, won't hear of it. I'm fine."

Ernst and I and the borrowed army vehicle lurched and wove through joyful celebrants. "Here we are, Del, not a scratch or dent on the vehicle. And you're at #12 in time for duty. Allow me a Puritan New Year's kiss, won't you, my dear?"

I offered a cheek, then fled to my cubicle to change for night supervisor duties. The full turmoil from Ernst's proposition appeared only after I lay down to rest.

# 47: Needed proof

I didn't sleep, nor was I awake. Questions, answers, and excuses looped and entangled themselves in my mental chatter.

*So green at my age, and after a year in a war zone? I'm still inept in personal matters. Damn!*

I chose to hear words only, not to evaluate the whole situation. Ernst's initial invitation was innocent enough. I thought our shared experiences had created a unique relationship between us.

Alas, I succumbed to flattery and the temptation of a New Year's Eve outing. And I knew Ernst didn't have to consider the cost. What did his declaration of love mean? I'm no more attractive than the plain Jane I've always been.

I wasn't interested in sex without marriage. I couldn't marry Ernst, and I didn't want to be married to him. He was too used to giving orders and he drank more than I could accept in a husband.

I didn't even know if I wanted to be married to Charlie, but I was in fact, even if no one else knew or would recognize our proxy papers. Complicated? Yes, my life was complicated.

On New Year's Eve I had let Ernst's proposition crack open a gate that controlled a vortex of physical need. I fought it, but Ernst and Charlie became one entity in my mind that night.

Memory of my erotic experience with Charlie overtook my body. I yielded to self-gratification, attacked myself with guilt, then wondered whether I would ever escape the attitudes to sex I'd been taught at home.

I prayed, "Send me a sign if Charlie is alive." I repeated, like a mantra, a rosary, or a comforting rhythm, "A sign, please, God," until sleep overtook me.

I didn't see Ernst at the New Year's Day dinner in our mess, but we often had different schedules so I thought little of his absence. The hospital's menu included ham with mustard and pickles, roasted potatoes and mashed turnip, followed by apple pie made with canned filling, and a fresh orange for each person. I enjoyed the cook's effort because I was used to a special meal on New Year's Day at home.

Everyone was sharing plans, expectations or fears for 1919.

"What about you, Sister Della?" a colleague asked.

"I want to stay in France for a while to help wherever needed."

I wasn't scheduled for surgery the first couple of days of the New Year and understood why when I overheard someone say. "We're going to miss Dr. Ernst. No one's left who can perform the reconstruction surgeries he did."

My gut went leaden. Ernst had gone, without an apology, or goodbye! I willed a message about Charlie to arrive, but remembered "God helps those who help themselves," a common saying in East Cove.

Matron sent me a memo the first week of January. "We're expecting a visit from the brass any day, so ensure the nurses under your supervision maintain our excellent standards."

I passed Matron's message on to my nurses and added, "If you learn the official or his car has arrived, kindly alert me right away. It always helps to have a heads-up." I intended to pass within view of his entourage, just in case.

I would have loved Charlie as before if news of him arrived. I needed proof he was alive, not a memory or an unfortunate dream, like my nightmare of the infant with her birthmark.

~

I was valued only for work when nurses were desperately needed. I knew our government was dumping nurses like broken crockery. Would I be next?

I decided not to return to East Cove, the spinster aunt expected to work like an unpaid scullery maid. I was not in a rush to face the Deacon, but no longer feared him. I understood his ilk survived by silencing, isolating and intimidating victims. I was grateful to the war for my increased strength; however, my gratitude did not extend to the Deacon.

I put my smile on for duty shifts, became calmed, then cheered, by men who thanked me for a sip of water or a clean bandage. Matron's memo had revived my hope.

I checked my mail box, and lingered there.

"Is there anything I can do for you, Sister Della? You're always doing favours for me," the reception nurse said.

"I'd be grateful if you'd let me know right away if anyone important drives up. Matron wants us especially sharp for the brass who are expected."

An orderly rushed up to me just then. "Sister, you're needed immediately in surgery. The scheduled nurse dropped, sick."

Duty came first.

"Welcome aboard, Sister Della," the surgeon, a man named Ellis, said, "I hope we haven't taken you from a tea party."

I scrubbed furiously, then set out sterile instruments, a little too noisily, and checked bandage and linen supplies. I started to set up a Dakin's drip.

"You're efficient today, Sister. Do calm down. With luck, we won't need the full surgery outfit. We're setting a broken leg with no skin lesions."

"Sorry, sir, I understood this was an emergency."

"It is, but not life threatening. Our patient was in acute pain. We'll have the x-ray result any moment and decide our course of action then....Looks like it's coming now."

He held up the x-ray, and pointed. "See here, right leg, both tibia and fibula are fractured, more like cracked. The fragments are in place, so we'll not disturb them. We'll give her a plaster cast to carry around."

"Her?"

"A nurse. She borrowed her fellow's bicycle."

I set out bandages and padding, and mixed plaster for a cast. An orderly rolled our patient into surgery. She'd already been given morphine to ease her pain.

First, we cleansed the affected area. She winced when we touched the leg with the slightest pressure. We wrapped her leg with padding, especially where the ends of the cast would be, and then applied a layer of wet plaster. It would harden as it dried.

She remained calm and told us about her ride. "I liked the feel of cycling, the air on my face, the thrill of going fast and faster. I veered into a rut to avoid a crash with a car that was coming at me, and fell over. My leg cracked when I hit ground. Shall I tell them at home it's a war injury?"

"If you add, 'almost'," I replied.

A desire for the thrill of cycling flooded me. "Any chance you could get your friend to lend his bike to me? I'd be careful with it."

"Sorry, Sister, I daren't ask. He's in trouble for letting me ride it. You see, he's a Kiwi and it's army property."

"Kiwi?"

"A New Zealander. They've a bicycle corps."

"Interesting." I smiled in relief when I heard the friend's nationality and renewed my plan to buy a bike one day.

Dr. Ellis advised our patient to have her leg checked frequently for colour change, and for pressure sores. He also said she might need another cast when the swelling went down.

He dismissed me with a "Thank you, Sister Della" as soon as I'd tidied up after our bone setting.

I rushed to reception, then to my cubicle for a cry. I had seen the back of an officer and his assistant, who were driving away in their army car.

I wished I'd never married Charlie. Did our intimacy matter, relative to the worse morals I'd witnessed in Europe? Charlie and I had created a dream world, but our proxy marriage had tied me down. I would be better off single.

The reception nurse tapped at the post outside my cubicle. "Sister Della, the major was in a rush. Said he'd come back for a proper visit after Etaples. It may be weeks, or a month."

*Damn!* My innards slumped and tightened as I struggled to retain composure.

"Thank you, Sister. You'll let me know when they come back?"

"Promise."

Early evening, I smiled at the lengthening sunlit hours, enjoyed a mess meal, even a watery coffee. Matron scheduled me less and less frequently for surgery assistance as the need diminished. By the middle of February, I was supervising only eight hours, six nights a week.

I tried to mix with other women. I attended a tea party. How strange it was to pass an hour in leisure without close friends or family. Petit fours and tiny sandwiches lacked appeal for me, though I admired the easy conversational skills of other women. Similarly, tennis matches seemed a fruitless use of energy.

I didn't comprehend such frivolity, but there was one activity that did interest me. An acquaintance wanted to see Etaples. "So many of the men have been there, for training or hospitalization," she said.

I recognized a perfect way to visit Etaples without standing out. "I've had driving lessons. Why don't we volunteer to transport supplies?"

Matron agreed. "As long as you don't miss a shift. I'll arrange an ambulance, and you may transport two stretcher cases who'd receive more appropriate care in Etaples. Here's a letter to introduce you to my colleague there. I say she may trust you with anything she needs sent to #12 General. You realize you'll have but a couple of hours in Etaples?"

I'd been hoping for more.

Etaples was overwhelming, like the hospital area of Rouen. There were a half dozen hospitals, hundreds of sheds. I inquired at each hospital's reception desk whether Charlie was registered as a patient. Results were negative.

"The lists of discharged patients only go back about a week," a sympathetic clerk informed me.

I realized it would take weeks or months for me to find Charlie if he had been in Etaples and discharged more than a week ago.

A few words with the major's assistant held greater hope of resolving my mystery. When would the major return?
During the next weeks, little irritations: snoring colleagues, not quite clean forks, improperly folded linen, were trifles overshadowed by my anxiety about the return of the brass and my messenger.

In March, Matron relayed orders from the American Army. "Sister Della, you're to assist me in demobilization of # 12 General Hospital."

I supervised preparations for transportation of patients until none remained. Next, I supervised packing the surgery equipment for its return to the United States.

I travelled toward Brest in anticipation of embarkation in later March. My heart was heavy. No hope of learning about Charlie's situation.

As I left the train in Brest, I caught a glimpse of the major with Charlie's friend who had visited #12 General the day I had assisted setting the leg bones. The crowd was dense, the pair a city block away.

The chance was slim, but I pushed my way through the crowd toward my prospective messenger. I saw him speak earnestly to the major, who nodded assent.

Charlie's friend came straight over. "Sister Della, kindly come with me. I have important information to share with you."

He led me to a small office in the interior of an army building, and closed the door. His face was grave.

"Please do sit down, Sister. Finally, we can talk in private. This is difficult for me because Charlie was a close friend." My messenger's eyes glistened. "What was your last news from him?"

"He was about to go to hospital in Etaples."

"Right. Charlie boarded the train to Etaples. Unfortunately, the train was bombed en route. Everyone aboard was assumed lost. The inferno melted glass and metal, everything."

I recalled the Canadian crew that was repairing the tracks to Etaples when I had passed with Henri and Drs. Ernst and Jones in December.

"Were other men from his group on that train?"

"Not many, but the fighting was fierce during our offensive. Most of the men he knew, his lieutenant, and padre, the whole detail, about thirty men, died in the trenches about the same time. A Flying Pig. The area's still a mess. The remains unidentifiable."

I sat stunned, tearless, wordless.

"Sister, there's talk of a monument for soldiers whose remains are unidentified. The idea is to have each man's name engraved on the memorial. Looks like it'll be in Ypres."

"Mmm."

"I've submitted Charlie's name."

"Mmm."

"He talked of you fondly and of the possibility of you having a life together. I'm so sorry for your loss."

My body shook. "Thank you for telling me. This was difficult for you."

"Sister Della, I can't leave you alone, but I must return to my major. I insist you accept a volunteer to see you to your boat. They're friendly, unobtrusive guides, used to the boarding routine."

"Thank you, for your kindness." Energy had left my muscles.

**Marie Mossman**

# 48: All I want

We headed out of the building, into the crowd. On the way, I heard a familiar woman's voice from the past, a lower class English accent.

I was puzzling who it might be while Charlie's friend engaged a volunteer. "A few minutes ago, Sister Della received bad news, so kindly accompany her to the boarding ramp."

He shook my hand. "Goodbye, Sister."

I must have appeared stunned, but my mind churned.

Did Charlie register our marriage anywhere that has survived? I'm glad to be single again, aren't I? No. I want Charlie alive and a proper marriage.

If the army was assuming his death, I could too, but there would always be a smidgen of doubt. I now comprehended the phrase 'shadow of doubt'. Total, one hundred percent freedom I would never achieve.

I didn't want to marry anyone but Charlie and vowed to bury myself in work. I volunteered as nurse on the voyage home. Helping others would become my therapy.

I recognized the coarse English accent during my first meal aboard the SS *America*. Bonnie had managed to arrange transport to the States, as a dining room server. I'd never dreamed of meeting her again.

"My 'usband's on the ship, too. A 'merican private. We're settin' up a boarding 'ouse in Boston. He's a cracker 'andy man, 'e is, and I kin cook the meals. I'm gonna make a better life in 'merica. What 'bout you, Sister Della?"

"Not sure yet, Bonnie. I'll nurse, wherever I can, but prospects are dim for nurses with the government laying us off."

"After all you nurses did for 'em!"

Another surprise awaited me when I reported for duty. A Midwestern accent intrigued me this time, Karen.

We caught each other's eye across our hospital ward of homeward bound patients. This lot of damaged bodies lacked the verve of the eager fellows I remembered on the *Olympic* headed to England, less than a year earlier. Karen greeted me with a smile and wave, and we arranged a tea break together.

"We only meet when travelling!" I said.

"Life on the road, or sea, that's us," she quipped. "What are your plans? Do you have a job lined up?"

"No, it's a worry."

"I don't have a job fixed up, either, but I'm not concerned. Father feeds lots of hospital bigwigs at his restaurant. He can arrange a position for both of us. How about it?"

"Are you sure? It'd be super if he could!"

"I'm positive, Della. And you must live at our place when you first come to Youngstown. My family's always having people stay while they get settled."

"I don't know what to say, but thank you. I'll come to Youngstown and apply."

"Super. My family won't understand what we've been through. No one could unless they were over there. It'll be a comfort to have you to talk to. All I want now is a normal life."

"Me too."

Bonnie and I exchanged a few words after she plopped stew on my plate one noontime. I told her about my hope of a job in Youngstown.

"Glad to 'ear. Knew something'd come up for you, Sister Della."

"Bonnie, think of settling in Malden. It's near Boston, smaller but growing. My cousin, Katherine, lives there, and I'm sure she'd help you meet friends. There's opportunity for rooming houses there, as much as in Boston."

"I'll talk 'bout it with my 'usband. Thanks, Sister Della."

# 49: At sea

*At Sea, off Brest*
*March 1919*
*Dear Katherine,*
*How is the weather this March? You, Frank, and 'little' Frankie, how are you all keeping? Healthy and warm, I hope. You must be happy we have Armistice before Frankie has reached enlistment age.*

*We're a day out of Brest, heading to the States at present, and the sea wind hits with a raw cold when I walk the deck.*

*I work regular shifts, nursing as a volunteer, on the voyage. My challenges remain depressed patients, Spanish influenza, and wound infections. My days plod by, similar to those immediately preceding demobilization of #12 General. I no longer sense adrenaline rushes like I remember at the casualty stations close to the battlefront. What will life be like after debarkation? My friend, Karen, tells me she knows someone who can arrange jobs for us in her hometown of Youngstown, Ohio. Am I foolish to believe he has influence to do it?*

*I've taken the liberty of mentioning your kind nature to Bonnie, a woman I met when I first arrived at Fargo Hospital in England. She travels on this same ship. (Confidentially, we didn't get on at first, but she's a fighter, a hard worker, and has a good heart under a rough manner.) She and her husband plan to set up a boarding house, and I suggested Malden as a town with a future, and went so far as to recommend she look you up because you are friendly. Please do what you can for her, and she'll fight for you if you ever have a need.*

*I'll visit as soon as possible, am so anxious to see you, but must go to Youngstown first, and settle the employment situation, if I can.*

*Do excuse my wobbly writing. The ship is rocking at present.*
*Sincerely,*
*Del*

My second letter was to my cousin in East Cove.

*At Sea, off Brest*
*March 1919*
*Dear Charlene,*
*I do hope you and George and the children are keeping well. It's soon time to dig up your parsnips left to sweeten over winter, and to plant sweet peas, isn't it? How I love their scent! Have you started some seeds inside yet? Is it lettuce or Swiss chard, you always have before the rest of the village?*
*You may have heard how difficult it is for nurses to find employment now our governments are demobilizing us. I'm lucky a friend on board assures me she knows someone who can arrange a job for me in Youngstown, Ohio, so I'll be going there directly from the ship. Apparently Youngstown is a growing community and has a new, well-equipped hospital.*
*This summer, if the dreadful influenza has passed, I should be free to come home, as I dearly wish, to visit, catch up on the news, and to breathe the sea air.*
*Until then,*
*Yours sincerely,*
*Della*

The third letter was to my brother.

*At Sea, off Brest*
*March 1919*
*Dear Dan,*
*I'm out of touch with the challenges you have faced this last year in East Cove. It'll be wonderful when you write a line to tell me how you, Bertha, and your boys are getting on. While*

*away, I've enjoyed a sense of stability from the thought of you in charge of the farm where we grew up, your farm now, but in my memory 'our farm'.*

*Your name and address will continue as my 'next of kin' contact, and, for a while army mail will come to you, until I secure employment. Let me know if it's too much bother for you to forward letters until I'm settled. Of course, I'll be back in summer, as soon as I can get a holiday.*
*Sincerely,*
*Del.*

I bought stamps at our ship's commissary and posted my letters at the purser's desk to go with others into regular mail in New York.

Marie Mossman

# 50: Youngstown City

In mid-March of 1919, our ship steamed up the Hudson.

Karen called out. "The Statue of Liberty!"

I cheered, jumped up and down, roared with the shipboard crowd. It thrilled me more than I had expected. I can only imagine how excited my American colleagues were to see their national symbol.

Karen and I kept each other in sight as we disembarked and passed through the gauntlet of immigration officials. A group of us in our white uniforms were lined up for a photograph in front of a cement building. For government propaganda? I've never seen a copy of the picture.

The most other attention we received was from taxi drivers seeking our trade. We hired a car to drive us to the train station.

"No line goes directly to Youngstown," the ticket agent explained.

We bought tickets to take us as far as we could and transferred to a different line for Youngstown. No one knew exactly when to expect us, so in Youngstown we paid another taxi for the short distance to Karen's home, where her parents welcomed me into their large stone house.

They had engaged an accordion player to entertain her extended family and friends. Her father's Italian restaurant staff presented a feast such as I'd never seen before; perhaps not as delicate as food I'd eaten with Ernst, but competitive for first prize in a different category.

Soon enough, the Youngstown City Hospital hired me for ward nursing. I took a room in the nurses' residence when one became available after a week.

Windows invited sunlight and fresh air when I opened them to my private room. The one-storied residence had a communal kitchen, and I could obtain meals at the hospital's cafeteria if I did not feel like cooking.

Karen and I went on adventures like browsing at Strouss', Youngstown's multi-storied department store. We'd check out shiny costume jewellery, or new coat styles, or have a malt. I remember my companionship with Karen fondly.

She invited me to her home for family dinners frequently on evenings when we were both free. I remember one occasion when her father was home.

"Della, what are you doing to save for your future?"

"I put a percentage in the bank for if I get sick, or my family needs help."

Karen's father pursed his plump lips and nodded his balding head. "Good idea, but you should invest for a better return. I recommend shares in a local company. I know several businessmen who donated to our base hospital when fundraising was going on, before the war, their own money, and I'd be happy to advise you. You won't regret buying shares in a solid local company."

I bought a few shares, not as an investment, but from gratitude for the wartime support. It was my farewell to the war.

# 51: I secured

*June 1919*
*Dear Della,*
*How is life in Youngstown? Tell me, I want to hear about the people you've met, the styles, and amusements.*

*Isn't it wonderful we can write proper letters without worry about censoring? I hope the government never again reads our mail. You wouldn't dream what I have to tell you about East Cove.*

*The Deacon is going around saying. "I'm a sinner. My limp is God's punishment." Can you imagine!*

*There's more. Our cousin Geoffrey is not the same since the war. He began painting houses, but goes on benders. I plan to give him work when the rain lets up, and the air is drier, and hope he isn't drinking then. I think both he and the Deacon have gone loose upstairs.*

*Our youngest, Maud, too. I so want her to finish high school like you and I did, but I can't talk sense with her. Could you consider, I know it is a lot to ask, but you helped out Katherine when she was confined, and you know the world better than I do. Della, would you think about taking Maud back with you when you come home in summer? She might listen to you because you have faced so much danger. You live in a calm manner, independently, with your own income. You would inspire her to aim higher. She has a good sense of humour, so you might enjoy her company. Please think about it. We can talk it over when you come home in July. The strawberries will be ripe by then.*
*Sincerely,*
*Charlene*


I reacted immediately to Charlene's request by renting rooms in a respectable house near the high school before I left Youngstown on holiday in July.

On my way to East Cove, I stopped in Malden to visit Katherine in her new house. She invited Bonnie and her husband for a roast beef and mash dinner the evening I was visiting.

"Katherine introduced us to 'er agent," Bonnie announced, "an' we've got our eye on a property already." Her smile was constant as she ate and chatted.

Katherine and I chin-wagged while we cleaned up.

"I thought you might come home with a husband, considering how many men were in France."

"I didn't."

"Don't tell me you didn't have your chances."

"I didn't go to capture a man, Kath."

"Their loss, if they couldn't lure a solid woman like you into marriage. How's Youngstown?"

"Booming, and I'm glad of a job. What are your plans for the house? It's big for the three of you."

"We're going to let out the top rooms to pay the mortgage. I don't like being in debt. Later, I'll move my sewing up there."

"You and Frank are doing well. I'm happy for you. What a blessing the war ended before Frankie had to go."

A scene of operating on a youth in the CCS flashed into my head, and I had trouble holding back tears, but I said nothing about it to Katherine.

"You look tired, Del. Let's go to bed so you're rested for travel tomorrow."

~

I travelled from Malden to Easton by car, steamer, and train. Dan picked me up at the train station. He hugged me so tightly I could hardly breathe.

"Del, you've come back! We're so happy to see you, practically your old self after the war!"

"Quiet, Dan. You'll have me crying."

We drove by horse and wagon along the old coastal road to East Cove.

"Rich people are buying cars, Del, but then they pay for petrol to fill the tank. Our horses trim the grass in the paddock, and are eager to take us visiting in Blandford or shopping in town."

"Both the old ways and the new have their advantages, Dan. I drove a truck last year. Zipped along at forty miles an hour for ages, and got to like driving. Seems like another life, now."

My mind wandered back to Ernst's lessons.

Dan and Bertha put me up in the borning room, converted to a guest room. I recognized one of Mother's crazy quilts on the bed, and noted a new window overlooking the back gardens. How peaceful, how much more at home could one be?

I went across to Charlene's as soon as politeness permitted.

"Oh, Del, how delightful!" She stopped sorting mail. "Mother's had me take over her postmistress job. I've held this letter in case it's for you. It's been misdirected different places, probably because of the writing. The return name looks like it may be a doctor E something, but the postmark is California..... Have a look."

I recognized the sender's name, thanked Charlene, and accepted the letter to read later.

"Are you still feeling the same about Maud?" I asked.

"I am, Del. It might improve her attitude to live away for a while. She's more restless than I was, more like you were, but not so keen on school."

"I understand, Char. I'd love to have her with me, and I've rented rooms in a boarding house close to the Ursuline High School. It only takes girls. We won't have to fuss about meals most days. A college for shorthand and other office skills is expected to open in Youngstown. I'll pay her tuition there for a year, if she does well with the Ursulines."

"You're so generous, Del!"

"I'm rather strict, you know. Maud'll have to co-operate, or I'll send her back."

"I'll make it clear to her."

"You keep her busy working in the garden and house this summer, and bring her, or send her with someone, to Boston in September. I can meet her there."

"I'll sleep tonight for a change."

"Good." I had another question. "You mentioned about the Deacon and Geoffrey in your letter. The Deacon always was funny in the head, and I'm not interested in seeing him. But tell me, Char, has Geoffrey done your painting?"

"Not yet. I expect him tomorrow. Come see him."

I walked over in the morning to say hello to Geoffrey. He stood on a ladder in the sitting-room and chatted with me while he brushed paint on the ceiling.

And then he stopped. We were alone. He looked directly at me, his eyes open only a slit, his voice quiet but firm. "I was in France with the army, too. I know your secret, Della."

My gut muscles tensed. My face froze, as calm and strong as I could make it. "We all have secrets, Geoffrey, even you."

He returned to chatting about weather and gardens while he painted. I wished him well in his chosen trade and left the sitting-room minutes afterwards.

~

While home, I discussed writing a new will with a lawyer in Easton. He said. "Since you have no children, Miss Schwester, think about what's important to you."

I had no need to ponder. "How can I encourage equal opportunity for women and men?" I asked. Then I added, "And decent health care." The legalese frustrated me, so I asked him to write a document for me to peruse later.

Afterwards, I bought a Raleigh bike with red trim. I used it for visits and fresh air outings, peddling around East Cove while there. Charlie's spirit set me free to live, so I secured Ernst's letter in my brassiere during my return trip to Youngstown. The possibilities of re-connection with Ernst warmed my heart.

# Postscript

Jean's daughter looked up to Della, older and straight of spine. They stood on a hillside field, under a clear summer sky decorated with puffy white clouds. The distant waters of Easton Bay rose or fell according to the Moon's attraction.

Della plucked daisy petals. "He loves me; he loves me not…"

Her eyes focused on something the child could not see.

**Marie Mossman**

# Acknowledgements

Thank you, Brenda Thompson of Moose House Publications, for taking a chance on my first novel, and Andrew Wetmore, Moose House's patient editor, for guiding *A Rebel for Her Time* to the finish line. Thanks to Moose House's art department, especially Rebekah Wetmore, for designing the book's appealing cover.

Kate Kennedy, independent editor, provided initial editorial input on the manuscript.

My husband, author of *Going Over: a Nova Scotian Soldier in World War I,* encouraged me continuously to write the story. He shared his knowledge of WWI, and of past coastal Nova Scotian society. My daughter read an early version of *Rebel*. She commented on the story, and provided the words that eventually became our title. Her partner also consistently encouraged my enterprise, as did my sons in their unique manner.

*Rebel*'s story benefited further from the encouragement and critiques of a community of extended family, friends and acquaintances. Whispering elements of some shared events may have found a home in the story.

Teachers Susan Halley and Judith Scrimger reduced my self-doubt and provided helpful comments about my writing. A bit of their DNA should be implanted in every teacher.

Members of The Wolfville and Area Newcomers' Writing group; Sobey's Writing Group, New Minas; and especially the Writer's of the Round Table encouraged me, shared information, and told me frankly when I erred or my phrases were awkward.

Librarians and archivists, close and distant, professional or voluntary workers, invariably responded to my requests for information. They are guardians of our history and culture, resources that may help us avoid repeating mistakes, personally, and as the human collective. A linguist pointed me to Dickens for creating British accents.

I'm grateful to readers who donated time from their own projects to comment on our pre-publication edition of *A Rebel for Her Time*: Sara Williams, author of *Growing Fruit In Northern Gardens*, with co-author

**Marie Mossman**

Bob Bors; Sue Kerr, author of *Unlikely Stories of a Perfect Childhood, A Memoir;* Laura Churchill Duke, author of *Two Crows Sorrow: Love and Death on the North Mountain*; and Jim Prime, author of more than twenty books.

Thank you all

*Marie Mossman*
*1 November 2020*

# About the author

Marie Mossman packed local stories and family secrets into her brain, when a child in Nova Scotia. She accompanied her parents on their drop-in visits to relatives and friends along winding main roads and dusty rural offshoots, by boat to island communities. The wistful stories she overheard mellowed in her heart. The more shocking ones remained in her brain. Elements of the childhood treasure trove have passed, transformed, into this novel.

Ms. Mossman taught school and practised speech-language pathology. Success in a contest with a non-fiction piece, "Gang of Three Canucks Hunts Peking Duck", encouraged her desire to write. She has participated in writing seminars, classes, and writing groups since 2010. She completed a series of articles for *The Grapevine*, a local newspaper.

Her more recent research for *A Rebel for Her Time* led her beyond paper and interviews to World War I sites in France and Belgium. Since 2017, she has focused on research and the ephemeral skill of writing with honesty, interest, and grace.